THE SCANDALOUS CONTRACT

The Dauntless Ladies Series

ELECTRA TANNY

KINGSLEY
PUBLISHERS

First published in South Africa by Kingsley Publishers, 2025
Copyright © Electra Tanny, 2025

The right of Electra Tanny to be identified as author of this work has been asserted.

Kingsley Publishers
Pretoria,
South Africa
www.kingsleypublishers.com

A catalogue copy of this book will be available from the National Library of South Africa

Paperback ISBN: 978-0-6398420-9-7
eBook ISBN: 978-0-6398420-8-0

Also by Electra Tanny

The Dauntless Ladies Series:
The Man I Love

My love as deep;
The more I give to thee
(William Shakespeare)

Chapter 1

London, 1825

'I understand you met with Lydia in New York,' Lord Eastwood said to John, the Duke of Rutland. To the sound of the words, Isabel slowed her pace.

Lydia, where have I heard this name before? Isabel thought and stopped short of entering the ballroom. She slipped to the side of the balcony and hid among the thick foliage. She cursed herself for her indecency, but something was amiss with John, her fiancé lately; she sensed that the two men's discussion would answer her questions.

'I did,' Isabel heard John admitting.

'How is she?' Lord Eastwood asked.

'She is thriving,' John answered, and Isabel caught the warmth in his voice.

Who is that woman? she wondered, and her stomach tightened in vile premonition.

'I am happy for her,' Lord Eastwood replied.

'You need to go to her. She is all alone over there with no one to protect her,' John said vehemently.

'I cannot, John.'

'Don't you love her?' John asked.

'I love her, but she doesn't love me as **you** very well know,' Lord Eastwood said. 'But even that is not what is holding me back here. I love her enough for two.'

'So, what is holding you back?'

'I am ashamed of myself. You don't know what I did. I don't deserve her.'

'Whatever it is she will forgive you. Go to her, fall on your knees, and beg for her forgiveness.'

'I can't forgive myself. I… betrayed her. I didn't defend her when Prince Alex made the most disgraceful and inappropriate advances towards her. And what is worse, I was blinded by greed, and I was contemplating the unthinkable. I was ready to hand her over to the Prince for my personal gain.'

To the sound of this John turned and grabbed him by the neck. Isabel gasped witnessing her fiancé's violent outburst, but she managed to contain herself and stand still.

'You filthy…' John spat.

'Kill me, I beg you,' Lord Eastwood pleaded. 'I deserve it and more. I have behaved abhorrently.'

Isabel was horrified. Her mind worked quickly trying to decide whether she should reveal herself and put an end to the madness. But luckily, John pushed Lord Eastwood away. He inhaled deeply trying to calm down.

'You don't deserve her but still, still…'

'Why don't you go to her. She loves you and I believe you love her too. I shall never bother you. I promise,' Lord Eastwood whimpered.

'She will not have me. I asked but she wouldn't accept me,' John said disheartened, hiding his face in his hands.

Isabel felt the ground retreat beneath her feet, her knees weakened. She had to leave. She gathered her courage and slipped into the ballroom. She walked with pace through the crowded room to find her parents. She couldn't breathe. She had to escape. When she found them, they swiftly took her home to her relief. And despite their worry, her parents respected her request to be left alone without seeking explanation for her sudden morose mood.

In the privacy of her bedroom, seated at the edge of her bed, Isabel allowed herself to make sense of what she had heard. Her fiancé loved another woman and had crossed an entire ocean to go to her. Her fiancé would have stayed with this Lydia person if she had asked him to. Isabel laughed, releasing her pent-up tension, while tears ran down her cheeks. And then, she collapsed on her bed weak from the humiliation and the despair.

The next morning, when Isabel opened her eyes, she felt quite differently, neither hurt nor hopeless and a new emotion filled the space. She was genuinely sorry for John. How miserable his existence should have been knowing that he would never be able to be with the person his heart truly desired.

At that moment she couldn't help but wonder what this other woman looked like, sounded like. What was it that made incredibly powerful men like Lord Eastwood and the Duke of Rutland, fall desperately in love with her. She stood up and looked at her reflection in the full-length mirror hanging on the wall opposite her bed. Her hair looked impeccable despite having slept on her tight chignon that made her head hurt. Her skin was flawless; always careful not to spend too much time under the sun. She practised fluttering her eyelashes and smiling modestly while ensuring the blue of her eyes remained visible. She did that perfectly too. She reminisced over her encounters with John. They enjoyed each other's company; of that she was certain. The man never showed a hint of boredom when conversing with her. She chose safe topics, such as the weather and his favourite pastimes. And John luckily had noticed and had gone on to further inquire after two unique objects; her grandmother's oriental vase and the little ivory statue of a sailor, that her mother had meticulously placed in their parlour. Both objects had interesting backstories that made an excellent conversation starter, and Isabel had made sure to memorise all the details. John seemed quite impressed with what she was imparting or at least she thought so. She never once displeased him by voicing any opinions on political matters. Not that she had any as she had always found such topics, which the menfolk basked in, exceedingly boring.

So, what was she to do? Were the duke's feelings strong enough to sustain their marriage? Would he be able to forget about this other woman and devote himself to her? And what about her own feelings? Did she love the man? The questions made her dizzy. She wasn't certain how she felt about her fiancé either. And how could she claim she was enamoured when he had left her for three months to travel to New York as soon as they announced their engagement. She hardly knew him if she wanted to be honest with herself. She only knew that he was the handsomest man she had ever seen; he was a duke; he was a good listener because he hardly ever interrupted her or said much in return. Confused she wondered what was she to do? Her parents were adamant. She had to marry for love.

She pressed her temples, trying to relieve the pain that had resurfaced. She felt like crawling back to her bed, but she knew well she had to dress quickly. John was certainly visiting her, as a devoted fiancé would do, after her quick exit from the ball last night and she was determined to speak to him.

Chapter 2

Nothing and no one could prepare Isabel and her family of the hubbub the news of the broken engagement would cause. The vicious rumours, wild insinuations and outright fibs shocked Isabel to the core. Unless there was a truly scandalous reason, no one would ever refuse a duke's proposal. The haute ton turned their backs on her and her family and revealed their contempt in any social occasion as if Isabel had committed the gravest sin. Men who had previously declared their undying love and admiration would not even gaze at her, let alone acknowledge her. Isabel found herself desperate, not only for herself but for her parents too, though they supported her decision completely. They asked Isabel to be patient convinced that the negative sentiment would ease overtime but as months went by there was no improvement.

Nothing was enough to change the ton's mind. Not even the daily visits of Catherine and Diana, the duke's sisters, to her home where they offered their ardent support.

'Isabel, please. You need to make an appearance at the next ball. We shall stand by your side and declare our support, including that of our brother of course,' Catherine begged.

'I thank you Catherine, but I doubt anything is going to change the ill sentiment of the ton at this moment. They will most likely praise the duke for his kindness towards the fallen, unworthy lady. Besides, I would not like to taint your reputation with my presence at your side. Didn't you notice the looks of contempt at the park the other day? Your championing didn't do much to appease their resentment.'

'We know what happened between you and our brother and you were clearly wronged. We want to help you. We owe you that much,' Catherine said, lowering her head in shame.

'Oh Catherine! You do not owe me anything. You both always stood by me like true sisters. You have nothing to feel ill about.'

'I do feel awful,' Catherine whispered with a sigh. 'Because I knew. I knew that my brother's heart belonged to another woman. I knew that he travelled to New York to go and see her before your wedding, and I didn't do anything to stop him. I just hoped that your union would remedy his broken heart.'

'You were protecting your brother. You have nothing to feel sorry about. I would have done the same if I had a beloved sibling. And you brother is a kind, honourable man. Do you know he renewed his offer to me after witnessing my fall?'

'He did? That is excellent. You should definitely accept,' Catherine said.

'I didn't marry your brother because he didn't love me. I shall not marry him now knowing he is pitying me.'

'Do not let your pride cloud your judgement, Isabel. Love is not a prerequisite to a happy marriage. Look at...'

Catherine stopped abruptly.

'Look at yourself,' Diana, her sister, offered, pointing at Catherine. Isabel's eyes grew round with horror.

'Oh no! Catherine, I had no idea!'

'Do not pity me, Isabel. I am the happiest I could ever be. Thomas is an impeccable husband. I highly recommend you look beyond sentiment and think of prospects. And with our brother, your prospects are sure to be excellent.'

'For heaven's sake sister! Just because you gave up on love you should not encourage others to do so. I adore our brother, but he made a grave decision for himself, and Isabel should not pay the price for it. At least Thomas worships you,' Diana said.

Isabel witnessed the conversation in silence still trying to process Catherine's bold admission. Her friend did not marry the man she loved. She would never have guessed. She always looked so happy by Thomas' side. And on her wedding day Catherine had looked radiant and determined, at peace with herself. How was it possible to tie herself for life to a man she did not carry affectionate feelings for?

'Are you in love with someone else?' Isabel asked in trepidation.

Catherine hesitated for a minute. She lowered her head.

'Tell her,' Diana urged.

'I do love someone. A man that I have known all my life, but he would never return my affection.'

'But, how can you know? You did not even give him a chance,' Diana protested.

'I did give him a chance! He is aware of my feelings, and he turned his back on me,'

Catherine shouted as tears filled her eyes. She, then,

covered her grief-stricken, flushed face with her quivering palms. Diana and Isabel looked at Catherine in shock. It was not for her to lose her equanimity.

'I am sorry, sister. I did not know,' Diana whispered and hugged her. 'I am so sorry. I will kill him.'

'You will not say a word to him. And we shall not speak of it ever again,' Catherine said decisively and with a wistful smile composed herself. 'I am happily married now. Thomas is kind, handsome, clever and he loves me. I am confident that I will manage to forget and return my husband's affection soon. In fact, I am very close to declaring myself utterly enamoured,' Catherine boasted only to be met by the thin smiles of her sister and Isabel.

Isabel cleared her throat. 'Anyway, the best course of action for myself right now is to leave. My parents and I are going to spend some time in Paris.

Chapter 3

Isabel, exhilarated, couldn't stop smiling the minute she stepped on the ship to cross The Channel. The traverse, however, was not the smoothest. The sea, in turmoil, raged against strong winds and currents. And while most passengers proved quite sensitive in their stomachs, Isabel was never affected and quite enjoyed the experience. She strolled on the ship's deck, with a steady footing, gazing at the sea's choppy waters and the solid land as it came into sight, feeling only regret that this adventure was approaching its end.

'The lass 'ere 'as a seaman's spirit,' Isabel heard an older sailor saying while untangling ropes. She felt flattered and valued his compliment as the best she had ever received.

I have a seaman's spirit, Isabel thought, and immediately dreamt of walking bare foot, in breeches, with her hair loosened on the deck of a ship. The image moved her, and she prayed for such a freedom in her life. What if she woke up in the middle of the night and had her little walk? Would it be dangerous? Her reputation could not be harmed any worse, could it? If only her mother knew what she was brooding over! Isabel giggled at her bold, erratic ideas. She felt the itch to be brazen but soon composed herself and dismissed the insanity that had taken over her. But still…

Is it possible to feel this happy? Isabel was overwhelmed looking at all the Parisian sites flashing hastily in front of her eyes as their carriage moved through the elegant Parisian streets. She never recalled feeling that happy at any of the balls she attended, not even on the day the duke proposed. *Have I ever loved this man?* She felt a nasty pinch in her gut and pushed the thought away. She didn't want to contemplate the matter anymore, eager to put the past behind her.

'I am so glad to see you smiling, my dear,' her mother said with relief. Isabel reached out and held her hand.

'Despite everything Mother, I dare say I have a good feeling about what lies ahead,' Isabel confessed.

Her father grunted through his teeth.

'Everything will be well, dear,' his wife offered but Lord Pearlbrooke wasn't content, and Isabel was well-aware of the reason. He despised the fact that he found himself obligated to his younger sister, Countess Thalia Bassett, whose husband tragically died only a couple of years after their wedding. The Pearlbrooke family was devastated with the demise of the man, not only because of the close ties they had with him but because he was the one person on earth who managed to hold sway over Lady Thalia, indulging her impulsive character. When Lord Bassett offered to marry her, the Pearlbrookes celebrated for taking the young hellion off their hands and moving with her to Paris. They were relieved that Lady Thalia's shenanigans would not taint the family's reputation anymore.

Lord Pearlbrooke would never risk Isabel being exposed to the ludicrous ideas and often improper behaviour of his younger sister, but he was left with no choice since Lady McDowell, his older sister, declined his request to receive them in Edinburgh when they decided to flee London. In her reply, she offered her sincere apologies, explaining she had her two unmarried daughters to think of who couldn't afford being associated with any scandal. Lord Pearlbrooke was deeply hurt but could not blame his sister for acting upon her daughters' best interests, though, Edinburgh was miles away and the news was not likely to spread beyond the limits of London.

'How long has it been since we last met Aunt Thalia?' Isabel asked her parents.

'She visited us after her husband died five years ago,' her father answered, shaking his head at the memory.

'Has it been that long?' Isabel was shocked to realise. 'It feels like yesterday.'

Isabel didn't quite understand her parents' discontent with regards to her aunt. She had heard terms like "blue stocking" and "rebellious" without really understanding what any of these meant and why they were objectionable. She vividly remembered that she liked her aunt a lot though she had indeed managed to shock their household upon arrival back then.

Isabel leaned comfortably back in her carriage seat, closed her eyes and dived into her memories. Thinking back, her aunt had been defiant, and Isabel smiled.

The fourteenth of May 1820 was the day the Pearlbrookes were receiving her mysterious aunt. Isabel remembered vividly that day and how she kept bombarding her mother with questions; what she looked like, what she liked doing with her spare time, but her mother sternly warned her, 'Your aunt shall not be disturbed, Isabel. Grieving widows are not inclined to any entertainment, and she will surely keep to her chamber for the better part of the day.'

Isabel was somewhat disappointed, but she was a sensible girl, despite her thirteen years, and understood the need of a grieving person to isolate though she had never experienced any loss herself.

When her aunt's carriage halted outside their mansion her parents and staff appeared mournful, Isabel observed. But when her aunt descended the carriage, all eyes widened and there were gasps. Isabel noticed her father blushing like never before while her mother's ashen face betrayed her horror. Isabel was simply mesmerised, unable to fathom the reason behind the commotion. All she saw was a beautiful young woman in a bright red gown who wore her hair up while loose tendrils caressed her cheeks.

'What on earth are you wearing?' Isabel heard her father whispering to his sister. 'This is highly inappropriate!' he scolded her.

'Not now, my lord,' her mother said.

Isabel was not given the opportunity to greet her. Her aunt was ushered inside and into her father's study. Isabel, intrigued discreetly moved closer to the study door and tried to eavesdrop.

'Have you lost your wits, sister? What are you wearing?' She heard her father, his voice raised, quite aggravated. Isabel did not ever remember hearing her father so upset before and she wondered whether eavesdropping was such a good idea, but her intrigue got the better of her and she continued to listen.

'I don't expect you to understand, brother. Please, allow me to grieve my husband how I see appropriate.'

'Appropriate? I can assure you there is nothing appropriate in this apparel!' he huffed. 'Under this roof I expect you to act with decency and good sense.'

Her aunt's thunderous laughter reached Isabel, and she was truly shocked. Who was this person who dared to laugh in her father's face? Isabel swallowed hard wondering if her aunt was truly deranged but a little part of her liked her mischievous nature already.

'Listen, brother. I can promise you that I will hardly leave this house. I have no shred of desire to socialise with anyone. However, you cannot dictate what I shall wear. I am deeply grateful to you for accepting me into your home at this time of grief, but may I remind you that I am not obligated to you. My late husband ensured my independence with financial means to last my lifetime,' she said, and it was the first time her aunt's voice broke. 'If this is too hard for you to accept, I would gladly take my leave right this instant.'

'Isabel!' Lady Pearlbrooke exclaimed.

Isabel turned round, mortified, to find her mother aghast with her, quite upset, her grip on her waist.

'Eavesdropping is highly inappropriate! Go to your room immediately!'

In all her thirteen years, Isabel had never been scolded and sent to her room before. She was always compliant and ready to please her parents, but she was not in the least upset for getting into trouble. For once in her life, she had witnessed a drama, and she rejoiced the fact that she would finally have something that was not excessively boring to impart to her girlfriends when they next were extended an invitation to meet.

From that day on, Isabel constantly tried to spend time with her aunt. She hid in corners of the house and waited for her to go in the library or in the drawing room but as soon as Isabel joined her, her mother, or a maid, would swoop in with an excuse to take her away. The intent was becoming so obvious that her aunt started tapping her hand against her thigh, counting the seconds before Isabel would be ushered away. Isabel joined in and counted along and the minute someone appeared at the door the two of them exchanged cheeky glances. In no time at all, it had become their little jest.

Day by day, Isabel was becoming exasperated. It was truly ridiculous that she was not allowed to spend some time with her aunt. She was a relative after all. The more they prevented her from being with her, the more eager Isabel became.

Peering outside her bedroom window one morning she glimpsed her aunt going for a stroll in the garden. That was the opportunity Isabel was seeking. She ran downstairs and discreetly slipped outside through the balcony doors of the parlour and followed the path her aunt had taken. She found her seated on a stone bench in an inlet among the thick leafage, weeping uncontrollably. Isabel, remorseful for intruding on her privacy, turned to leave discreetly.

'Blast it all! I forgot my handkerchief,' her aunt swore. Isabel halted hearing her vulgarity, blushing, yet something inside her flickered like a flame. She hesitated and then realised the least she could do was to offer her handkerchief. She moved slowly towards her aunt who was trying to dry her eyes with her sleeves. The sound of a breaking twig underfoot made Isabel jump and attracted Thalia's attention.

'Hello, Isabel,' Thalia said with a wry smile.

'I have this,' Isabel said. She passed her handkerchief avoiding eye contact with her aunt and made to leave.

'Don't go my dear. It is alright. You can stay with me a little while.'

Isabel sat reluctantly next to her. 'My mother said that I should let you be in peace at this grievous time.'

'Your mother is very obliging and caring. Though I cherish my loneliness, sometimes I need to be in the company of my keens.'

Isabel exhaled with relief. She didn't want to impose. 'Are you crying because of your loss? I heard people saying that you are not really mourning,' Isabel blasted out, instantly regretting her forward question, her cheeks burning.

Her aunt giggled. 'Some people can't see beyond the obvious, unfortunately. I know what the consensus is for a grieving widow. They all expected that I wear black and hide behind a veil, but I would be dishonouring my husband if I did that. My husband loved seeing me in red gowns and wearing my hair in a loose chignon. Though, he is not among the living anymore, I truly believe he is still with me, around me. I can feel him everywhere and I want him to see me at my best, just as he did during the time we were together,' she said and sniffled into the handkerchief.

Isabel could see reason to her aunt's argument. She was aware already that appearances did not always reflect one's emotions. She contemplated, for example, her mother's resentment every time Lady Marrey called, only to wear her most radiant smile and appear perfectly content while the two ladies had their tea together.

'Who is to say how one feels? Appearances are deceiving sometimes,' Isabel stated.

'There might be hope for you, niece.'

'Hope? What do you mean, Aunt?'

'Nothing, do not mind my mumbling.'

'So, you did love you husband,' Isabel sighed with relief.

'Ardently,' Thalia admitted.

'My parents say that love between a married couple is the single most important thing.'

'Well, I am truly surprised, I must admit. I never thought I would agree with my brother on anything. I hope your parents will stay true to their word and spare you the agony of a loveless match, my dear girl. For your sake.'

Her aunt's words sounded ominous.

'Isabel!'

Thalia and Isabel looked at each other. Thalia put her finger in front of her mouth signalling to Isabel to stay quiet. They waited silently and watched as the maid walked past them, both aware that if they were found together in the garden, her parents would not be pleased.

'Now, go,' her aunt urged her quietly after the maid had safely disappeared.

'Three hundred and sixty-eight,' Isabel said before she walked away, and Thalia furrowed her eyebrows.

'The number of seconds passed before they came looking for me,' Isabel whispered.

Her aunt burst into laughter unable to contain herself. Isabel bit her lower lip fearing they would be discovered and started running back towards the house.

The day her aunt was saying her goodbyes, Isabel tried to seem unaffected. But when she turned her back on them and started descending the stairs of their mansion to her waiting carriage, Isabel ran after her. Ignoring her startled parents, she fell into her aunt's embrace.

'I will miss you, dear Aunt.'

'I will miss you, too,' she said and gave her a tender peck on her cheek. 'You have fire in you, my girl. Don't let anyone tame it.'

To this day Isabel had no idea what her aunt's words meant back then. Maybe now it was a good time to find out.

Chapter 4

Paris, 1825

'Welcome, welcome!' Lady Bassett exclaimed with open arms seeming truly happy to receive her guests. Isabel noticed how her eyes lit up when she took notice of her.

'Let me take a good look at you, Isabel. My God, you are a true beauty.'

Isabel blushed and curtsied to greed her aunt.

'A curtsy? Come here you silly,' her aunt said and hugged her tightly.

'I am very happy to see you, Aunt Thalia,'

'Thalia, Isabel. Please call me Thalia. I am not that much older than you, I am merely eight and twenty,' she said with a smile. Isabel looked at her parents and her father nodded approvingly but when she looked back at her aunt, she discerned a hint of disappointment in her eyes that Isabel was not sure how to interpret. But she knew that she had plenty of time to delve into her aunt's enigmatic thoughts.

The next morning Isabel woke up early and rang for her lady's maid. She got dressed quickly and rushed to the breakfast room. She couldn't wait to start her day.

She was really looking forward to visiting the Louvre, the infamous Parisian museum that her friend Helena visited a few years before and she swore it was the best thing she had ever experienced in her life. When she entered the breakfast room she was taken aback by the serene ambiance and gentle beauty of the room's décor and furnishings. The beige, heavily flocked wallpaper and the earthy, muted colours of the furniture's upholstery, soft and richly plush, was unlike anything she had seen before. For a few minutes she forgot about her day's plans and set to admire the unique art on the walls that depicted exotic places with tall swaying palm trees, feral animals in bright hues of orange and yellow and colourful wildflowers in green meadows; beauty unknown to her.

My mother will adore this room, she thought, and she couldn't help wondering where everyone was. She waited for a couple of minutes, surveying the solidity of the highly polished wooden tables and consoles, but her tummy was rumbling so decided to break her fast alone. The variety of food laying on the table in front of her was overwhelming. Boiled eggs, kippers, different flavoured cakes of different sizes, a plate of rusks, golden-yellow butter sitting in an ornate butter dish, a colourful array of fresh and dried fruit filled a basket.

Obviously, her aunt went above and beyond to please her brother and his family. She tapped her fingers against her lips trying to decide what to have. The variety confused her. She wished her mother was with her to help her with the choice. She decided to have some eggs as she did everyday though she was craving a big piece of chocolate cake that made her mouth watery. Her mother would never allow her to have cake. She always advised Isabel to be careful with her food choices and keep her waistline slender. They had spent a small fortune in ordering her gowns for her coming out and any alterations would mean more time and money. *Not that it matters anymore, does it?* she thought to herself and the idea of having a little taste of that delicious dessert seemed inevitable.

She quickly trotted to the drawing room door and stuck her head out to see if anyone was coming. No one was in sight. She, then, focused her attention to listen for any steps in the distance. Again silence. She smiled to herself and hurried back to the table. She picked up the knife and licked her lips in anticipation. As the knife cut through the fresh cake, Isabel debated what to cut next. She was being brazen and her tummy churned with excitement, but she couldn't but feel a bit guilty too for her insolence. Thus, she curtailed her appetite and cut a small piece. Besides, there was so much food to sample from.

The first bite melting against her tongue made her sigh audibly. She closed her eyes to savour the sensation and threw her head back. The flavour and texture were divine. Her stomach growled, a clear sign that she needed more to satisfy her craving. She finished her small piece in no time, and she decided on a second. She observed how all her guilt had quickly evaporated with each mouthful, and she cut a generous piece the second time. When she finished that too, she licked her lips, leaned back in her chair and rubbed her tummy. She was stuffed but had enjoyed it immensely.

And then, a bleak thought crossed her mind that made her open her eyes wide. She was always such an obedient, and obliging daughter to her parents and loyal to her friends. She always tried to do the right thing, and, in the end, what was she left with? Nothing! All her efforts to secure a husband and live a decent, respectable life were in vain. And she couldn't help but wonder what she had been missing all this time. What other pleasures were out there? Maybe, she should have eaten more cakes, drunk more wine and been bolder. She could have followed a beau secretly into a garden to experience more kisses. She blushed profusely at her wicked, secret fantasy but still she didn't regret it. Excitement coursed through her, quite uncharacteristically.

She, then, thought of her kisses with John. She had to confess she enjoyed the sensation they had brought to her a lot. Being in the arms of this strong, handsome man made her feel warm and fussy in unspeakable places. She dared to admit that she missed him. Did she make a mistake by not marrying him? A nasty pinch in her stomach made her hug her tummy, her crossed arms across her front. The warmth offered her some comfort. If she had married him, she would have been a well-respected duchess, with a handsome, powerful man at her side. Her parents would have been at home enjoying the company of their friends. Due to her stubbornness and her bruised ego, they were all punished she thought, and her lower lip started trembling.

But then her mother's words came to mind: 'Blessed are those who feel well-loved by their spouse.' Thus, no. She couldn't regret her decision. She could never have married a man who didn't love her. What if she fell for him and he was incapable to ever return her affection? She shook her head with resentment. She would have been miserable. She knew it well. In an unlady-like manner she wiped her nose with her sleeve and pushed her shoulders back. She had to compose fast because at any minute her parents could walk in. She didn't want to upset them anymore.

Where is everybody, she wondered again out loud starting to worry. It was not for her parents to wake up late. Something was amiss. She decided to go and find them just as Thalia entered the room.

'Thalia! Good morning. Have my parents already taken their breakfast?'

'Your father is a bit unwell this morning. He woke up feeling feverish. We summoned the doctor, and he will be here soon.' Isabel paled with the news. 'Oh no! Do not be alarmed, my dear. His symptoms are not serious. He didn't even want to call the doctor. I insisted. After my experience I do not take matters of health lightly,' Thalia added, sounding regretful. Isabel remembered that her uncle had died of a failed heart. Did her aunt feel she could have prevented his demise in some way?

'Come. Let us go upstairs to see for yourself,' Thalia said encouragingly.

Isabel was relieved to see her father. He looked well despite his fever.

'I am sorry my darling for disappointing you, but we will not be able to visit the Louvre today,' her father said disheartened.

'I could still take Isabel to the Louvre,' Thalia suggested. 'We could leave right after the doctor's visit.'

Lord and Lady Pearlbrooke looked at each other and both hesitated to answer. She wiggled uncomfortably in her chair, and he cleared his throat.

'Aren't you tired Isabel? You must be after our long journey,' he intoned clearly expecting his daughter to take the hint and avoid the outing with her aunt. But Isabel was determined.

'Not at all Father. I feel perfectly rested,' she answered with an innocent mien noticing how Thalia pressed her lips trying to supress her smile.

'Right. Then, I guess it will be good for you to go.' And turning to Thalia said, 'But please do not be late back.' Isabel noticed his tone and furrowed eyebrows.

'I guess your parents are afraid I might corrupt you,' Thalia commented with a chuckle, as soon as they closed the door behind them.

'Which doesn't not make sense, knowing that my reputation is already in tatters,' Isabel said shaking her head.

Isabel was really taken both by the artefacts of the museum and by Thalia who was giving her the tour.

'I must confess. I am very much impressed with your knowledge.'

'Thank you,' Thalia said, 'I have always been particularly interested in art and history and I read anything I can get my hands on. Do you enjoy reading?'

Isabel blushed a little feeling self-conscious. 'Not particularly, no. I have studied a little history and geography but only as much as it was required.'

Thalia raised an eyebrow. 'Any special interests, then?' she asked.

'I used to draw a little.'

'Have you abandoned your past time?'

'I had to. Preparing for my coming out was quite time consuming.'

Thalia hmphed exasperated. 'Oh, I remember that dreadful time. I simply could not withstand wasting my time on learning all these rules of conduct and names and titles of all the illegible bachelors. I felt my brain was slowly dying,' she said, giggling.

'You are right,' Isabel admitted. 'I devoted all my time learning, always being meticulous and it got me where I am today,' she remarked with distaste.

'Well, your situation is not that adverse, Isabel. You are in Paris, visiting one of the most beautiful museums in the world.'

Isabel chortled. 'I guess it could have been worse. I could have been trapped in a loveless marriage as we speak,' Isabel confessed.

'Lady Bassett!' The two women halted and turned to the direction of the call.

'Lord Girard! Welcome back. I am very happy to see you,' Thalia answered.

The stunning man bowed in front of the two ladies. He looked straight into Thalia's eyes ignoring Isabel. He took her hand in his and pressed his lips in a lingering kiss without breaking eye contact. Isabel noticed the fire in the man's eyes and swallowed hard. These two shared a secret and Isabel knew it was not a decent one.

'I missed you, mon amour.'

'Hush, Jonathan. People will hear,' Thalia protested.

'Lord Girard, let me introduce you to my niece, Miss Isabel Pearlbrooke,' she said but the man was not willing to take his eyes off Thalia. He was devouring her.

'Happy to make your acquaintance, my lady,' he said hastily.

'Now, Jonathan, don't be r...'

'I want us to renew our contract,' he interrupted her.

'Jonathan! This is not the right time nor place to discuss such matters.'

'I will pay you a visit later today then.'

'I have guests. My brother is visiting. I cannot see you today.'

'Thalia, please,' the man pleaded. 'I did some thinking while I was away. I love you. I need you in my life. I want a new contract with no ending date this time. *Lifetime* would be the least I would accept.'

Thalia stood frozen looking at the man who was obviously tortured by her silence.

'Jonathan, you know I can't.'

'Nonsense!' he snapped. He leaned in closer to her ear, but Isabel could still hear him clearly.

'I know how you feel, my love. You desire me too. Every sigh, every moan of ecstasy, the way you pant underneath me, is the proof.'

Isabel blushed profusely hearing his words. She knew she had to step away, but her damn legs stayed rooted on that very spot. She wanted to hear more. She felt that for once she was witnessing sentiment. *Is this how an enamoured man would look at me? Is this how he would speak to me?* She thought of the duke. She never saw him looking at her with such intensity. He never talked about feelings or desire. All the signs of his indifference were there, and she was too ignorant to recognise them. Thalia side glanced at Isabel looking worried. The man finally got the hint.

'I am so sorry, Thalia. I made you feel uncomfortable. I must apologise to you as well, my lady, for monopolising Lady Bassett,' he said, facing Isabel for the first time. He was a handsome man, and his mien exerted power and confidence, but his eyes betrayed the pain her aunt's dispassionate responses inflicted.

'Jonathan, I promise you. We will speak soon,' Thalia said, giving him a sweet, encouraging smile. The man bowed and walked away with lowered head.

'I am very sorry, Isabel. His behaviour was despicable. I hope he did not offend your sensibilities, my dear,' Thalia said.

'My sensibilities are intact. Please do not fret over it,' Isabel reassured her, and Thalia signed with relief.

'How could I be offended when I hardly understood what Lord Girard was referring to; ecstasy, moans of pleasure, something about panting…' Isabel went on explaining and Thalia's eyes grew huge, and she let out a choking sound.

'My God! My brother was right. I corrupted the girl within the hour,' Thalia exclaimed truly frightened. 'Please, do not repeat any of these words to your parents. My brother will kill me and there is no court in this world that will not vindicate him.' Isabel burst into laughter and soon her aunt joined in. 'You should have seen your face. Pure terror,' Isabel said, patting Thalia's back.

'That was cruel of you,' Thalia added, still tittering, 'So you know,' she added with relief.

'I do. Mother and I had "the talk" to prepare me for my wedding night. Well, mostly she did the talking. I wouldn't dare to ask her any questions on the matter. I was so embarrassed; I wanted to die.'

'But still, even I can recognise that what you have just witnessed was indecent.'

'It was real,' Isabel answered. 'Please, Thalia. I need to understand. Do not shy on me. What this man said to you, the way he looked at you, shed a little light to my lacking understanding on the matters of the heart. And I have so many questions. Please Aunt, I beg you,' Isabel said, tears welling up behind her eyes.

'Alright, I will answer your questions. What do you need to know?'

'His eyes. The way he looked at you. Was that love?'

'That was lust,' Thalia answered.

'Are these two different notions?'

'Yes. Sometimes they co-exist which is marvellous when it happens, but they can be experienced separately. You can feel just love for a man or you can lust for him. And sometimes lust can be quite deceiving and can easily be mistaken for love.'

'This sounds ever more complicated,' Isabel huffed. 'Do you suspect that Lord Girard suffers from such deception?'

'I am afraid he does,' Thalia admitted, looking pensive for a few moments. 'Anyway, Lord Girard's feelings are not of importance right now. So, what happened between the duke and you?'

'He admitted to me that he is in love with another woman, but he was still willing to wed me. But I couldn't…' Isabel said.

'Did you know who that other woman was?'

'No, I didn't know her. She is a businesswoman in New York.'

'A businesswoman? Oh my! I think I like your ex-fiancé a lot.'

'Pardon?' Isabel asked quite shocked.

'He is a unique specimen of a man I have to admit; self-assured and willing to accept a strong, unconventional woman by his side. Remarkable.'

'Well, they cannot be together. She is married. He was

in need of an heir, and he liked me enough to make me his wife. Do you think I should have married him?' Isabel asked in trepidation.

'Did you love him?'

'I thought I did. He is devastatingly handsome. He is very polite, and gallant and he was the only man that completely ignored me for quite some time. I couldn't understand his indifference then. Why did he ignore me while all the other men seemed utterly taken by me? I got obsessed with him. I wanted to win him over by any means. Thus, when he finally noticed me, and he offered for me I felt victorious. But, after breaking our engagement, I didn't shed a tear once for losing him. Thus, no I did not love him either. Maybe, I would have loved him one day but not yet.'

'I am happy you realise this.'

'You already knew my feelings? How?' Isabel asked.

'How can you love someone else when you don't love yourself?'

'I don't love myself?' Isabel asked. What was Thalia saying?

'What is your favourite colour, Isabel?'

'My favourite colour? What does that have to do with anything?'

'It has to do with everything. So, tell me.'

'My mama says that lilac looks good on me...'

'Dear God,' Thalia muttered, 'What is your favourite colour, niece? What colour gives you peace or excites you? What colour dominates your dreams? What is your favourite food? Which dance do you prefer? Such simple questions.' Isabel began to understand her aunt's point. She lowered her head. 'I do not know,' she whispered.

'What did you say?'

'I do not know,' Isabel repeated louder this time, reaching up to wipe away small droplets of sweat forming on her brow.

'How do you expect anyone to really know you and eventually love you when you don't know and you don't appreciate your own self, my dear girl. Our society has women believe that beauty is all it takes to lure a man into offering marriage. You have an excess of beauty, my dear and offers of marriage will come your way. But you claim you need more, don't you?' Isabel nodded.

'I do. And thank you, for your compliment.'

'It is the truth, Isabel. I didn't flatter you. I just stated the obvious. You do know that you are uncommonly beautiful, don't you?'

'Well… I am tolerable I suppose.'

'Tolerable? Do you even look at yourself in the mirror? Look around you Isabel. There is not a single man who doesn't pin you with his eyes. You are ravishing, my dear.'

'You are exaggerating now surely. For example, Lord Girard did not even acknowledge me.'

'That is because I am ravishing too,' Thalia declared and Isabel gasped hearing her boasting with such ease.

'Don't look so shocked, Isabel. I like me. I don't expect anyone to tell me if I am beautiful or not, what my virtues and what my flaws might be. I know all that already. So, when a man declares his love, I can recognise whether his affection is genuine.'

'So, that is how you suspect Lord Girard's love declaration may not be of consequence,' Isabel stated, realisation colouring her features.

'Precisely. We didn't have much time together. He does

not know all aspects of me. We need time. Now, it remains for me to decide if I am willing to give him that.'

'The contract. What was that?'

'You really do pay attention,' Thalia said and giggled. 'That I will not impart with you, my dear girl. I will only tell you that it is my way to keep all my lovers' emotions under control.'

'Lovers?' Isabel said with her eyes wide open.

'Oh dear! I think I have said too much already.'

Isabel was lost in her thoughts during their carriage ride back home.

'Blue, blue is my favourite colour, in all its shades and tones,' she said suddenly breaking the silence and sighing with relief. 'Also, I prefer eggs to kippers, I enjoy strong coffee more so than a milky tea.'

Thalia nodded approvingly.

'And I need books,'

'On what?'

'Anything; everything; And I want to go the theatre. I suspect I would like it.'

'You only suspect?'

'I have only been once when a suitor invited me. I remember I enjoyed part of it, but I was so anxious to look perfect that I really didn't pay much attention.'

Thalia roared. 'Theatre it is, then.'

When they arrived home, Isabel found Lord and Lady Pearlbrooke in the parlour. He no longer seemed to be suffering of any ailment, and her mother was at ease.

'Father! I'm so happy you are up and out of your bed,' Isabel said and she hugged him tightly.

'You look happy, my daughter.'

'I am, Father, very happy indeed. I had a glorious day, today. I am starting to see things differently.'

Her father arched an eyebrow and looked at his wife worryingly. She shrugged her shoulders closing the book she had been reading from on her lap.

'What do you mean, dear?' her father asked, hesitating a little.

At that moment, Thalia entered carrying a stack of books.

'Oh, brother you are up. I am so relieved. Isabel, here are some books for you. I gathered you a good sample of everything. Start with these few and we will discuss them after you have read them.'

'Thank you, Thalia,' she said with a glint in her eye. She took the books out of her hands, gave her a little peck on the cheek and rushed off eager to get to her bedroom. But her father's upset tone addressing her aunt brought her to a halt. She stood quite still behind the door and listened silently.

'What is the meaning of all these books, Sister? What have you done to our daughter?'

'I haven't harmed her in any way, Brother. I just helped her realise one simple fact. She doesn't know who she is.'

'What's this nonsense?' he bellowed. 'My daughter is perfect. There is nothing more for her to learn.'

'Perfect? In what sense, Brother? She is beautiful but what else can you say about her that recommends her really?'

'She has the sweetest disposition; she is kind, decent and compliant. And one day, she will be the perfect wife to a deserving man. I will make sure of that.'

'And?' Thalia asked.

'And, what?'

'All you have to say about your daughter is that she will make a good, compliant wife to a man one day? You filled her head with all this nonsense about marrying for love and you honestly believe that she will win a man's heart just because she is kind and decent? The poor girl is cudgelling her brain to understand what went wrong with the duke. She thinks that all it takes is to flatter your eyes a certain way. Meanwhile, she doesn't even know what her favourite colour is.'

She stopped for a second to catch her breath and then…

'Your sister is right,' Lady Pearlbrooke interjected.

'And… excuse me? Did you just say I am right?' Thalia sounded really surprised.

Isabel's mouth also dropped on hearing her mother vindicating her aunt.

'Wife?'

'Your sister is right my lord. Let me remind you, dearest, that we did not marry for love. Yet we were blessed with like-mindedness and our love grew so much that we only wished that our daughter would have the same fate. All we did, however, was to follow the conventional route. We trained our daughter like any other debutante though we wished for her to achieve something different. We both know very well that love matches are rare. Thus, what did we really hope for? A miracle?' she said, sniffling her nose into her laced handkerchief.

'Please, don't get upset. We will fix this, my dear,' he said. Isabel was crying too hearing her mother's regret. *Enough with the tears. Time for action,* she said to herself and ran to her bedroom, her steps light so as not to be heard.

Isabel was on a quest. She wished to find her true self. She started reluctantly by asking simple questions and she was resolved that her answers would be unbiased by the general consensus. The answers she got, were not always convenient. She shockingly discovered that she hated the light-coloured gowns, young, unmarried ladies had to wear. She learned that she felt more comfortable, and confident in garments heralding dark yet vibrant earth colours. She did not enjoy the merriment of minuets. She preferred the intimacy and the sensuality of a waltz. She also became an avid reader of all literary genres just to finally admit to herself that she enjoyed love poetry, sonnets, and romance novels. She was a true, romantic soul.

Theatre and travelling were pursuits she absolutely adored. And thankfully, her parents consented to both with great generosity. They travelled to Germany and Italy. She was blessed to watch productions of German Wanderbühne and the unique ballet performances in Nuovo Regio Ducale Teatro alla Scala. She attended a smattering of opera shows in Italy as well, but she found the high-pitched voices of the performers irritating.

She met new, interesting people and she boldly looked into their eyes searching for their truth. And the more she got to know herself, the easier she found it to interpret other people's emotions and intentions. She could see indifference and boredom behind the smiles of content in ballrooms; she could understand and feel the heat of lustful eyes watching her. She felt satisfied when she discerned men and women's surprise once they realised that she was more than a pretty face; that she did indeed possess some quality of mind. She enjoyed the nods of approval, admiration and even jealousy she sometimes inspired.

She did not particularly enjoy political discussions, but she would boldly offer her opinion if she found herself firmly fixed on a belief. She felt knowledgeable and confident but there was only one thing that she didn't have the blessing to witness on her quest. Love and lust, combined in rare unison in a man's eyes. It was the only sentiment that would convince her to the altar. And though she felt relieved that she knew what her life goal was, she feared that she might never experience the rare sentiment. She knew she would not come across of any such display in ballrooms, where raw, true feelings were wilfully hidden. *Would I even be able to recognise them, she wondered?*

Chapter 5

'So, is it decided? Are you going back to London?' Thalia asked.

'It is time,' Isabel answered with a sigh. She knew she had to return eventually though staying in Paris and enjoying Thalia's tours in the Louvre and their captivating life discussions were what she would rather do.

'But why now after nearly three years?' Thalia asked.

'My parents are weary. They never complain but I can see it. And I received this,' Isabel said and passed a letter to Thalia. Thalia read eagerly through the inked lines. Her lips formed a small "o" of amazement.

'Oh my! What a scandal! Not only your ex-fiancé's lover is back but she has his two-year-old son with her? That absolves you in the eyes of the haute ton, for sure.'

'That is what Catherine believes too, and she insists I returned immediately. But I am not that convinced. How many would even bother making the connection?'

'You don't need many, my dear. Just a few will be enough. And if the duke's sisters insist on supporting you and maybe the duke himself, people will relent. As much as I hate parting with you, this is the best time for you to return to society.'

Isabel agreed silently. She was lost in her thoughts until she saw a sculpture so provocative to her senses that she was forced to a breathless standstill.

'I do not recall seeing this before,' she said.

'Breathtaking isn't it. It is called "Psyché ranimée par le baiser de l'Amour" by Canova.'

Isabel walked around it wide-eyed, taking in every inch of the two naked lovers, Eros lifting his woman, Psyche, in a protective embrace while she sank back with abandonment craving Eros's kiss. Everything was there, love, passion, and sacrifice carved into a slab of otherwise lifeless marble.

'Tell me more, please,' Isabel asked unable to take her eyes away.

'You ought to read Apuleius' *Metamorphoses*. Psyche was a mortal with infamous beauty that even Venus was jealous of. Eros was sent to kill her but instead he fell in love with her and married her after he made her promise she would never look at his face and reveal his identity.'

'Preposterous. I can't believe she agreed to that,' Isabel commented.

'They become passionate lovers until one day Psyche is tempted to break her promise. She takes an oil lamp to have a closer look at her husband and injures him mistakenly by spilling hot oil on his face.'

'Oh no!' Isabel exclaimed frightened, her hand to her chest.

'Eros flies away and Psyche sets off on a quest to find him enduring the cruellest tasks set by Venus. The last one is to go to the underworld and bring Venus a dose of beauty from Proserpine.'

'As if Venus was in need of more beauty while

compassion was what she truly lacked,' Isabel snorted.

'Vanity, my dear, sees no limits. Anyway, Psyche once again being curious, opens the box which deceitfully contains infernal sleep. When Cupid finds out about the fate of his wife, he decides to forgive her and saves her with a kiss.'

'Thus, once again, a woman was punished for disobeying a man's rules and her salvation depended on his benevolence,' Isabel remarked shaking her head.

'You just spoke like a true bluestocking, my dear,' Thalia giggled. 'However, I do sympathise with Eros's feeling of betrayal.'

'But his demand was absurd. Who wouldn't want to see their lover's face?'

'A promise is a promise. Psyche shouldn't have agreed in the first place if she felt incapable of committing to such a demand. He probably had his reasons; he obviously needed time to feel he could trust her before offering himself completely with no constraints.'

'Are we still talking about Eros and Psyche?' Isabel asked arching an eyebrow.

'I am getting married.'

'My lord!' Isabel squealed with excitement. She hugged her aunt tightly overwhelmed by the news. 'I truly thought you had given up on love.'

'I was determined not to endure the agony of tying my soul and my existence to a man's. However, fate had different plans,' Thalia said with a sweet smile.

'Who is the luckiest man on this earth?'

'Lord Girard. I believe you have met once. He persisted all these years, enduring all my caprices and I can safely say he has seen all of me, even the darkest side of my

character. He fought relentlessly and has won my heart.'
Isabel was unable to speak, so full of emotion was she.

'I hope I will come to experience such grand feelings one day,' Isabel confessed with a sniff.

'What do you aspire to find in your future husband?' Thalia asked.

'I want a daring man who will be sincere and generous in declaring himself to me. A man with a traveller's heart who would take me on the wildest adventures around the world, unrestrained by the propriety of our society. Of course, he has to be obscenely rich to afford such leisure and show such contempt to the ton's dictations. And did I mention handsome? But not in a trimmed and polished way. I want him to look savage and rough with no care if his hat is shiny enough and his clothes to be of the latest fashion.'

'I believe, my dear, you are seeking a pirate.'

'Yes, a pirate! With a natural propensity to cleanliness of course,' Isabel jested.

Chapter 6

It had been a week since Isabel returned to London, and she was unsure of how best to rejoin society. Catherine and Diana visited her almost every day discussing different possibilities. The two sisters insisted that Isabel should join them on their outings, signalling, thus, their support, but Isabel was sceptical. She was truly amazed to see that the duke and his new duchess's reputation seemed to be unscathed by their scandal despite its epic proportion. Not only was it obvious that the Lord Eastwood's widow had a son that resembled remarkably the Duke of Rutland, leaving no doubt who the boy's father was; they, also, got married almost immediately not even allowing a six-month period of mourning since her late husband's demise. There were some whispers of condemnation, but they were hushed hastily as no one would dare displease the powerful Duke of Rutland. And yet Isabel was striving for the ton's acceptance for merely deciding on her fate and future. She felt truly repulsed by their hypocrisy and cursed her need to be welcomed by their lot. *How the hell did they do it?* Isabel thought to herself.

'Who are you referring to?' Catherine asked. Isabel blushed profusely and bit down on her lower lip realising her blunder.

'Did I say that out loud? I am so sorry. I was just wondering how your brother and his bride didn't suffer any consequences,' Isabel answered resolved to address the matter openly if she wanted to claim she was any different from the rest of her peerage. Catherine shrugged her shoulders. 'I guess my brother is very powerful,' she offered quite uncertain of the veracity of her response since they had all witnessed the mortification and crash of powerful families over the years for scandals far less serious.

'My brother and Lydia didn't care about the ton's opinion, and they demonstrated their indifference in any way possible. That forced the esteemed members of our society to think hard before reacting and to realise that any confrontation or slight would leave our brother unaffected while the perpetrators of gossips would likely find themselves in a precarious position. If John and Lydia showed a shred of fear or regard to the ton's sensibilities, they would have been slandered relentlessly,' Diana said while rolling a chocolate cookie in her hand which she devoured as soon as she stopped talking.

'I believe you are right sister. What an insightful observation!' Catherine said quite amazed and spent a couple of minutes in contemplation of her sister's words.

'Now I know what needs to be done!' Catherine exclaimed with a sigh of relief.

Catherine refused to reveal her plans but a couple of days later Isabel received an invitation from Catherine to join her and Diana for tea. Isabel felt quite nervous finding herself in the duke's residence. What if he showed up?

How would he react to her presence? How would she feel if he saw him again? And worse, what would she do if she happened upon his Duchess? It was quite insensitive of Catherine to invite her there, but Isabel could not turn down the invitation. Catherine and Diana had shown her hearty support, and she wouldn't like to offend them.

When she entered the drawing room to join her friends, she was immediately stricken by the presence of a woman she had never seen before. A knot formed in her throat, blocking it and she tried hard to make the uncomfortable sensation go away. It was her; her "nemesis" and she was absolutely breath-taking. Isabel tried to hide her distress and smiled cordially but her cheeks were burning.

'Isabel, I would like you to meet the Duchess of Rutland,' Catherine said, looking at Isabel encouragingly. Isabel curtsied unable to stop gawking at Lydia who in return welcomed her warmly. The four ladies sat down at a round table where tea had already been served in pretty floral China and a plate of tiny, sugared pastries adorned an equally pretty three-tier plate stand. For a couple of seconds, they all stayed silent.

'Well, this is awkward,' Diana offered, in an attempt to break the mood.

'Diana!' Catherine scolded her, rolling her eyes. The sisters' exchange caused giggles amongst them and Isabel instantly felt some of the tension leaving her body and she began to relax.

Hesitantly, Lydia and Isabel started conversing, mainly talking about Isabel's travelling and then, Isabel felt compelled to inquire about Lydia's business ventures. Isabel felt a growing admiration for the woman and saw how John had fallen hopelessly in love with her.

She felt a pang of jealousy. Lydia not only possessed a rare beauty, but she was also confident, passionate and exerted a power rarely revealed by a woman so openly and unapologetically. She was the perfect duchess. Isabel found that she would very much like to call her a friend one day but a little something still bothered her. Lydia seemed completely unaffected by Isabel's past involvement with her husband and that wounded Isabel's feminine pride.

'Good morning, ladies,' John said, rushing into the drawing room bringing with him a gust of cold air and a bright smile which more than made up for the room's drop in temperature. The four of them stood up, one by one, and offered him a warm welcome.

Isabel had forgotten what a handsome man he was, and she felt a warmth in her heart seeing him again. When he realised, she was in the room, he approached her with unrestrained and obvious merriment.

'Isabel! What a nice surprise!' he exclaimed and gave her a tight hug that took her by surprise as she didn't remember John being so effusive. He asked politely after her parents, and they exchanged pleasantries, but it quickly became evident he was getting restless. When he turned his attention to his wife the atmosphere heated up. They exchanged meaningful glances but for a split-second Isabel could swear she saw a little glint of envy in Lydia's eyes which was all she needed to feed her vanity.

'May I have a couple of moments with my wife, please?' he asked without taking his eyes from hers. Lydia did not wait for an answer and moved towards the exit holding his hand. They were the embodiment of marital happiness.

'They simply cannot keep their hands to themselves,' Diana whispered.

'Diana!' Catherine scolded her once again puffing in exasperation. Isabel chortled. She had missed her friends so much. 'Your brother looks deliriously happy,' she said.

'He is. I am so glad fate brought them together. Nothing and no one could ever give him such rapturous joy,' Catherine professed but then she realised her blunder and turned instantly red.

'Catherine!' Diana scolded her obviously enjoying the opportunity she got to point out her sister's misstep.

When Lydia returned, her cheeks were flushed and her lips swollen. She took a couple of minutes to compose herself, anxiously running her splayed fingers through her untidy hair and tucking the strayed tendrils behind her ears.

'Isabel, would you like to take a turn with me in the garden?' Lydia suggested.

The two women walked outside in the beautiful garden the length of which stretched uncommonly for a residence in London. Isabel would have loved to explore it but now she was just curious to hear what Lydia wanted to speak to her of. They took a narrow stone path, quite secluded, and Isabel understood that their discussion was of a very private matter. She waited patiently allowing Lydia time to gather her thoughts.

'Catherine made a request of me which I think is quite fair,' Lydia stated.

'A request?' Isabel asked. Lydia cleared her throat. 'To help you. Both, John and I feel remorseful for the adverse effects our relationship has had on you. You have suffered greatly at our entanglement. John was truly shocked to witness the unfair slanders and gossip you had to endure, and he never forgave himself for not being able to prevent your fleeing. But we are determined to help you in any way possible, to re-enter society, if this is what you so desire,' Lydia said, and she lightly held Isabel's hand offering her reassurance.

'I am truly grateful to receive his Grace's and your support, but I would like to reassure you that leaving London was the best thing that happened to me,' she said smiling. 'I admit I was truly hurt when I saw people who once adored me treat me with contempt. But at the same time, I was relieved to have escaped a loveless marriage. And during my self-inflicted exile I discovered something valuable. Myself. And now more than ever I feel confident I will be able to get what my heart desires. A passionate, forever-lasting love like the one you and the duke are sharing.'

'I admire you, Isabel,' Lydia confessed.

'You admire me?' Isabel giggled quite surprised.

'I do. You were very bold to move forward and turn an adverse situation to your advantage. I am absolutely certain you will find the man of your dreams.'

'First we have the challenge of successfully convincing eligible bachelors to dance with me,' Isabel joked but her heart squeezed at the thought there was still a chance she would face the ton's slight.

Chapter 7

The dreaded day had come. Isabel looked at her reflection in the full-length mirror. She was content with herself. She chose her favourite gown in an earthy emerald green that looked remarkable on her. She would certainly make a statement with her choice. If any suitors approached her today, they should be well aware that this lady had changed. She was not an ignorant debutant anymore. She was a confident woman who didn't feel the need to conform to what society expected of her—*at least not in fashion*, she thought and smiled to herself. *But what if no one dares to ask me for a dance?*

Isabel swallowed hard remembering the humiliating moments she endured three years back. From being the most desirable dance partner, she had become invisible. No one acknowledged her or her parents. Young suitors stopped calling in on her and lifelong friends pretended they didn't see her, disassociating themselves with her, avoiding her company. Isabel's stomach tightened and she felt quite nauseated. Why did she even bother with these people? She secretly hated the idea of coming back. She even suggested staying in Paris with her aunt, but her parents were truly shocked with the suggestion and, besides, Isabel was not sure it was a good idea to be around the newlyweds. So, that had been her only true choice and she now had to face her reality with courage. She pushed her shoulders back and joined her parents in their waiting carriage.

'So, I understand you are to open the ball with the duke today,' her mother said, seeming as sceptical about the plan as she was but Isabel managed to veil her doubts.

'Yes, the duchess feels that it is the best way to signal their endorsement. They will welcome us and take it upon themselves to reintroduce us to society,' Isabel said, biting the inner side of her cheek.

'This is very generous on their behalf. We are really grateful but still… opening the ball with your ex-fiancé? Under the circumstances I am not sure it is the right approach,' Isabel's father offered.

'I know, Father. But I can see the benefit and the honour bestowed on me. And I cannot allow my fear to smother me. If this plan works, I will be content; if not, we will face what comes. But I am confident of one thing. The Duke and Duchess of Rutland will not give up on me.'

The carriage came to a grinding halt and Isabel observed she felt no fear any longer. An electric exhilaration had replaced the now fumbling fear. This was a new challenge in her life, and she now competently possessed the qualities she needed to claim her heart's desire. When she stepped outside her carriage the sight took her breath away. She had never seen the duke's residence decorated in such glamour and luxury. Fresh spring flowers framed the imposing doors and further decorated the long corridors and each of the rooms. The ornate candelabra and crystal chandeliers were all lit up and the chalking ballroom floors exhibited the most elaborate and fine art. Isabel was astonished by the grandeur, but she surely couldn't believe all the decorations were executed in her honour.

Her father's remark confirmed her observation. 'I believe a special celebration is taking place here today,' he said and smiled to himself.

'Isabel!'

Isabel turned to see Catherine and Diana and sighed with relief. The two women, with wide smiles, greeted Isabel's parents cordially and then Catherine coiled her arm around hers.

'There is a small change in our plans for the evening,' Catherine whispered surreptitiously. 'My brother is still offering to dance with you, but you will not dance the very first dance together,' Catherine finished saying in a hurry before she had to face the arriving guests, greeting them with smiles, all the while never leaving Isabel's side.

Isabel, truly relieved with the news, could now enjoy herself. She sensed the many side-on looks and heard the whispers mentioning her name as she glided through the crowded room, but she didn't care. Somehow, her confidence soared, and her spirits were lifted, and she had a very good feeling for the night's outcome. As soon as she reached the centre of the grand ball room, the duchess came to her with welcoming arms.

'Lady Pearlbrooke, I am so happy you were able to join us,' she exclaimed and kissed her on both cheeks. The intimacy of her actions raised some eyebrows but surely had a positive effect as Isabel's parents were immediately after surrounded and welcomed by old acquaintances. That made Isabel truly happy. However, she noticed that none of the bachelors presented themselves to fill their name on her dance card. She was momentarily disappointed but the acceptance of her parents by the haute ton was enough of a triumph for the night.

More relaxed she began observing the many guests now filling the room. She spied the old familiar faces of women who used to call her "a friend" and yet made a true effort to avoid her gaze this evening. Some old suitors were also in attendance who back then had sworn their devotion and forever lasting love. She sensed some anticipation on their behalf as they stared at her. Some made little steps towards her and then, mid stride, halted, obviously reluctant to make her reacquaintance.

The most refreshing sight was that of the new debutants who were visibly under stress but quite excited, oblivious of the viciousness of the race to the marriage mart. And, finally, the wallflowers; women who didn't manage to get the attention of the lot, who remained quietly subdued on periphery, lining the decadent walls. At that very moment Isabel felt envy. She would like nothing more than to be invisible, silent at the back of this glorious room, observing the theatrics and perfectly staged performances of the men and women attending. *Now that would have been so much fun,* she thought but her instincts told her that she would not have the privilege. At least not that evening.

'Ah Lord Sidmouth! You are finally here,' Isabel heard Catherine announce in a slightly irritated tone.

'I am sorry ladies, I was delayed. Miss Pearlbrooke, delighted to see you again.'

'Lord Sidmouth,' Isabel said with a curtsy and truly content on seeing him. He was the duke's best friend and Isabel remembered him being a delightful man, thus, she couldn't understand Catherine's annoyance.

'Make haste now. You know what you need to do,' Catherine urged him and Isabel looked between the two trying to understand.

Michael looked quite flushed. He extended his hand towards Isabel in a quite dramatic motion and opened his palm pointing at her.

'Well?' he asked, looking at Isabel.

Isabel stood motionless trying to read the meaning of the gesture which deliberately attracted attention.

'Your dance card,' Catherine offered and nudged Isabel's side. Isabel presented her card, but Lord Sidmouth took his time with it.

'First dance,' Catherine whispered.

'Isn't it already promised?' Lord Sidmouth asked obviously having been already informed of the family's plan. Isabel could not help feeling embarrassed. The only man who offered to dance with her was being forced into it.

'Lord Sidmouth, you don't need to do this,' Isabel mumbled disheartened.

'It is my pleasure, my lady,' he answered, giving her his most radiant smile and his answer seemed sincere.

'If you are being delayed, I promise you this will be the last time you will have the chance to dance with Isabel,' Catherine warned him sternly.

'As if bachelors will line…' Isabel didn't finish her sentence; a hoard of men, surrounded the spot she stood, clamouring for her attention.

Chapter 8

Isabel opened her eyes and sighed deeply with relief. She was in her bed, alone and took a minute to enjoy her privacy. But then she noticed her aching feet. In the past, she would have celebrated the sensation, considering it the welcoming aftermath of a triumphant night. It was true. She had danced the whole night. She received the most attention from all the marriageable women. All it had taken was for Lord Sidmouth to make the first move and then men rushed to her side. The initial plan had been aborted , thus, and she never got to dance with the duke. She was indeed disappointed for not having one last dance with the man. Not that she desired him. No at all. But she wanted perhaps to show him she was not an ignorant young woman anymore and it would definitely have given her a little break from the frivolous, uninspiring discussions she had otherwise had to endure the whole night. Any attempts on her behalf to deviate from trivial topics were immediately shut down by every man she danced with.

And then the "scandal" of the night. The dance of the duke with his duchess. Two people, in love, who didn't care to mask their true emotions proved too much of a sight for the majority of their esteemed guests. Isabel observed how their bodies were not inappropriately close; their hands only lightly touching. However, the heat in their gaze was a testament of their passionate love. That was all it took to offend the sensibilities of the ton. The whispers almost buried the music. The women frantically fanned their flushed faces intently as the couple twirled around the dance floor. Most men pretended not to heed notice.

Isabel had found the opportunity to observe the young men who seemed interested in her that evening. Most of the eyes looked empty but in one pair of eyes there was merriment; Lord Sidmouth's eyes, had sincerely enjoyed the sight of them. *Finally, a man who is not scared of true emotions,* Isabel thought to herself but then she observed something more. His eyes left the dance floor for a split second and his gaze fell on Catherine. Isabel saw it all, passion, love, pain. And Catherine must have felt it all too as she bowed her head only to compose herself a minute later and continue chatting, seeming truly carefree. He was the man her friend was talking about. He was the man Catherine was in love with and, what was even worse, he was in love with her too. *Why,* Isabel thought, and her tummy tightened. Why were those two turning their backs on such a glorious feeling? Isabel, confused, knew well she could never question her friend about it without inflicting pain. She had witnessed Catherine's desperation on the day of her admittance.

Truly baffled by matters of the heart Isabel started preparing herself for the inevitable stream of visitors. Eligible bachelors were expected today after her appearance. While her maid helped her into her morning gown, she lost herself in her thoughts.

'My lady, you do not seem content this morning. Is it the choice of your gown or maybe your hair?'

Isabel looked in the mirror. Her hair was braided in a very loose chignon and her morning dress was the simplest of gowns; exactly as she wanted it to be.

'No, I am very content indeed with my looks this morning,' Isabel replied. 'I need my guests to see my true simple self.'

Isabel had decided so the night before; she would not make any extra effort to dazzle her suitors. She was going to welcome them in her everyday apparel, compelled to challenge them with her honesty. *Gentlemen, this is who you will break your fast with,* she thought and smiled to herself.

'Either way, my lady, you look very beautiful.'

'Thank you, Esther.' Isabel replied and she found that she agreed with the observation. She too found herself beautiful despite the previous night's escapade. She finally started to love herself and that made her hopeful that a man would also come to appreciate and love her for who she was.

Isabel was not surprised to find the corridors and the family's parlour full of flowers. She had seen this sight a few years back, but the same excitement no longer filled here. Now she knew well that the gesture of offering flowers was nothing more than a part of a well-planned courting ceremony that meant little to the true feelings of the bachelors. However, there was a small bouquet of wildflowers that attracted her attention. Heliotropes and lavender, the most unique combination she had ever seen, tied together with a piece of brown string. Isabel laughed and her heart filled with warmth. Someone had actually made an effort in picking flowers for her. *How unique and thoughtful*, she thought. She immediately started searching the bouquet for a card. *Lord Emerson*, she read but she could not recall the man. Quite intrigued and with her spirits lifted, she entered the drawing room in haste.

As soon as she walked through the door, she was taken by surprise by the number of guests already waiting for her. Men smiled at her cordially making a little way for her as she moved towards her mother. Isabel observed the men trying to recall each of their names but there was only one man she was truly interested in talking to this morning. The presence of so many bachelors felt more like a hindrance than a blessing. Her mother, however, over the moon, smiled from ear to ear and her cheeks were rosy.

'Ah Isabel! Always punctual my dearest girl,' she remarked a little louder than she ought to, obviously trying to promulgate her daughter's virtues to the men surrounding them.

'Mother, do you know who Lord Emerson is? Is he here?' Isabel whispered in a conspiring tone.

'Emerson? Yes,' her mother answered arching her left eyebrow a little.

'Is he here? I need you to introduce him to me.'

'Lord Emerson?' her mother asked sounding a bit baffled. 'Are you sure?'

'Yes mother, please. Where is he? I cannot recall dancing with him last night.'

'Well, you didn't,' her mother responded reluctantly but Isabel didn't care to investigate her mother's feelings. She was just getting restless. 'He is there. By the fireplace…

the blonde gentleman talking to Lord Sanders. You must remember Lord Sanders. A delightful young man and you did seem to enjoy your dancing together,' her mother remarked but Isabel did not pay much attention. She craned her neck trying to take a good look at the man, but it was impossible with all the guests blocking her view.

'I need to talk to him,' she said and started moving intently towards the man her mother had pointed out. But as she was approaching, she got a better look at him. Lord Emerson was a stout young man, with unruly blond, curly hair that framed his face. Isabel sensed the disappointment creeping into her soul, but she was determined not to let the unpleasant feeling take over. *Looks aren't everything after all*, she told herself. Perhaps his mind would be enough to charm her and certainly his deed revealed a man of taste, dare and great imagination. She pushed her shoulders back and put on her brightest smile.

'Lord Emerson,' she exclaimed. The young man turned in her direction and his eyes grew wide as his mouth formed a small "o". *Oh Lord. He looks like a frog!* Isabel thought but immediately scolded herself for her rudeness. She determinedly continued to trot towards him.

'Lord Emerson! I am so glad to make your acquaintance,' Isabel said, giving the man her warmest smile.

'You are?' he said with a stammer but quickly composed himself. 'I am very happy to meet you my lady,' he said and took a bow before her. He then looked up at her unable to utter one word.

Very shy, Isabel thought, *but sensitive souls are expected to be shy, no?*

'Your flowers Lord Emerson...' Isabel began to say.

'Oh no! I am so sorry my lady if I offended you. It

was not my idea in the first place. My cousin, that idiot, suggested it. I had no time to order flowers for you as I had to collect my cousin from the port, and then my mama said that I have to be here today and I didn't know what to do, so he stopped the carriage and jumped over a fence, and he stole those flowers. Oh gosh, he is a thief, and the flowers are his loot, and I am so embarrassed to admit,' the man said and with a trembling hand he dried his forehead with his hankie. Isabel tried to make sense of the man's mumbling. *So, it was not even his idea*, she thought disappointed.

'So, your cousin had the idea?' Isabel repeated.

'Yes, it was all him,' the man repeated desperately.

'Lord Emerson do not get upset please,' Isabel said in her sweetest tone trying to calm the tormented man. 'I loved the idea of the garden flowers,' she said.

'You did?' Lord Emerson repeated quite baffled. 'But… but they were stolen,' he uttered.

'Stolen? They were handsomely paid for.' A deep guttural voice was heard behind Isabel's back that sent shivers down her spine. Isabel turned slowly and the sight of the man standing behind her took her breath away. He was the tallest man she had ever met in her life, with the broadest shoulders and darkest brown eyes. His skin was sunburned. His hair was longer than usual and slicked back in a hasty attempt to look presentable. His lips were luscious and full. Isabel envisioned herself nibbling them. She quickly shook her head from side to side trying to dispose of the lusting image that set fire to her body.

'A pirate,' she whispered, and she turned immediately red.

'A pirate?' he repeated and guffawed.

'I am so sorry sir,' Isabel said apologetically, 'but my comment is meant as a compliment really,' she admitted and grinned, continuing to examine his face more boldly this time, and spotting a little earring.

'A compliment?' he asked and smiled back at her revealing the whitest set of teeth Isabel had ever set eyes on. 'Are ladies allowed to openly pay compliments to men nowadays? I guess I have been away for a long time,' he commended, moving a little closer to Isabel who found herself rooted to the ground.

'As long as thieves are allowed to wander free and not get punished for their deeds, women can pay compliments. It's a crime a lot less serious, wouldn't you agree, sir...'

'David, David Longborn, Viscount of York at your service,' he said, and he looked into her eyes intently. Isabel instinctively bit down on her lower lip.

'You said that you paid for the flowers,' Isabel remarked.

'I did indeed,' David said, and he burst into laughter making Isabel's heart beat faster. 'I jumped over the fence, and I landed right in front of the landlady. I scared the life out of her. The poor woman turned white, almost found herself fainted.'

'Oh dear!' Isabel exclaimed, waiting to hear the rest of the story.

'I introduced myself and I explained to her that my dire deed was driven by desperation. That I had just returned from a long trip, and I was on my way to meet with the woman I was marrying but I had no flowers to offer to her. She was moved and helped me pick them. I offered her reward for her kindness. She only accepted because the flowers were going to my bride, and she thought it would bring good luck to her daughter if she added the sum to her dowry. As you see my lady, we now have to get married.'

'We have to?' Isabel asked and felt her cheeks burning.

David moved even closer to Isabel; in no doubt the distance of their bodies would no longer deem appropriate by anyone observing them. Isabel did not step back. All she wanted was to touch the man, but she knew better. She stood still waiting for his next words that made her feel giddy.

'It's imperative now. Otherwise, we will both be responsible for the ill fate of a young, poor woman whose good luck depends on our union.'

Isabel burst into laughter, and she felt the whole room looking at her, but she didn't care. She knew well in her heart that she was looking at her future husband.

Chapter 9

Isabel was lost. She lost her mind from the first second she laid her eyes on David and her obsession only grew stronger every time they got together which was practically every day. Every afternoon at two o'clock David would come to her doorstep in his barouche, and they took long rides together talking about everything; their travels; their adventures. Isabel even confided in him the scandal she had to endure a few years before and, to her relief, David seemed unaffected by it. There were a few random touches and prolonged looks, but David never tried to kiss her though Isabel's maid would wander off whenever they were seated amongst the blooms of the beautiful parks they customarily visited, when the weather permitted.

A desperate need began to haunt Isabel. It clung to her like a leech, not letting go. What if David didn't find her equally desirable though she swore his eyes betrayed the exact opposite. She looked herself in the mirror. She was glowing. Her parents told her so too. She was elated and distraught at the same time. She felt overwhelmed with the emotions that poured into her soul every time she thought about him. She was in love. She knew it well, but she did not know if he felt the same and that devastated her.

A reluctant knock on her bedroom door interrupted her thoughts. She looked hastily at the wooden clock on her boudoir to check if the time to see him had come but her special clock disappointed her, telling her it was still not time. The clock was one of her favourite items; she had purchased it in France and had insisted on having it on display in her bedroom despite the low ticking that most people would find annoying, but not her. The sound relaxed her, often lulled her to sleep, and reminded her of the transformation she experienced in a time of agony. She had to show it to David, but could she ever get him in her bedroom? The cheeky thought made her blush. She heard the gentle knocking at her door again.

'Enter,' she called, though she needed her privacy, to collect her thoughts and form a plan of how to discover David's true feelings about her. Her mother entered the room and Isabel sensed her unease.

'Isabel, my dear, I need to have a word with you.'

'What is it, Mother? Is everything well with Father, with you?'

'Yes, everything is well with us. We are worried about you.'

'About me? For whatever reason?' Isabel asked, suspecting that she wouldn't like where this discussion was heading.

'Your father and I want you to be truly happy, my love and we do believe Lord Longborn can offer you that. However…' She stopped and looked at Isabel, worry etched across her gentle features. 'There has been some talk,' her mother admitted lowering her head. 'People see you and the Viscount of York together every day since you met a fortnight ago and you do not accept the offers of outings with any other bachelors, so it is natural to assume that you and Lord Longborn have a commitment. Is it the case?'

Isabel lowered her head.

'No Mother. Unfortunately, David hasn't offered for me yet,' Isabel admitted, and she felt her tears welling up.

'Oh dear. Do you think he intends to propose?'

'I cannot be sure, unfortunately. He once mentioned that we have to get married, but he was jesting I am afraid. Oh Mother, I am so confused. Why does it have to be so complicated?' Isabel exclaimed and burst into tears. Her mother moved to her side and embraced her warmly.

'My dear girl, what are you saying? Do you love him?'

'I do. I have never met anyone like him. He is smart, considerate. He has travelled the whole world. And I am certain he has feelings for me. I can see it in his eyes; but he hasn't even kissed me,' Isabel admitted.

'I see,' her mother said, looking pensive. 'Maybe he needs time. You can give him that, but you also need to protect yourself. You have been through a scandal before. You know how hard it can be on everyone and especially on you. Maybe you should accept to meet with other suitors as well to signify that there is no engagement, and you can still see Lord Longborn but not as often to avoid presumptions. And in case he doesn't intend to offer for you, you still have some choice left for you. How does it sound my dear? I know it is not the most optimal solution but …'

'You are right, Mother. I shall do exactly that. We did receive an invitation from Lord Sanders for the theatre, didn't we. Maybe we should accept,' Isabel said. She was not interested in seeing any other man but David, however, her mother was right. She had to protect herself and her family from slanders and insinuations.

'Ah I almost forgot. You have a letter from your aunt.'

Isabel grabbed the letter with excitement and ripped the envelope open. She had been waiting for Thalia's response with great anticipation. She had enthusiastically written to her the very first day she had met David and confided in her all her thoughts and detailed information on the man. Handsome, obscenely wealthy, world travelled. She was certain Thalia would approve of him and had hoped she had a word of advice on how to lure the man. When she finally got to unfold the letter, she was shocked to see only a one-line sentence:

What is he running away from?

'You are very quiet today. Is there something wrong?' David asked looking worryingly at Isabel. He, then, raised his hand and felt her forehead for a couple of seconds. Isabel blushed, wishing he wouldn't stop touching her, but David pulled his hand away as if he got burnt.

'I am well,' Isabel muttered, feeling weak on her knees and quite disappointed from the short-lived physical contact between them.

'Or you are maybe bored of my stories,' David jested.

'I love your stories!' Isabel protested and *I love you,* she thought. And then she decided it was the moment to get bolder. She couldn't stand the anticipation any longer. 'Your wife and children are going to be the luckiest people on earth, enjoying your adventurous narrations.'

'My wife? I am never getting married,' David admitted. Isabel felt dizzy hearing the admission. Her lungs were suddenly deprived of oxygen, and she thought she would faint.

'Isabel, I….' He started saying but he halted obviously aware of her frustration.

Isabel inhaled deeply and took a moment to compose herself. The man was not interested in her. This was nothing. All this time they spent together meant nothing. The realisation hurt her immensely.

'David, I am going to be very honest with you. I love spending time with you. I enjoy every single moment, but I can't see you every day anymore. People have started talking and presume that we are engaged. We are not. I need to accept offers of outings from suitors,' Isabel said and looked sidelong to observe David's reaction.

David lowered his head, and Isabel could swear his breathing quickened. *Is he upset*? she wondered. The silent moments which followed were remarkably the most deafening Isabel had ever experienced. Never in her life had she wished for someone to stay silent, but she also craved his voice, his thoughts. She could clearly see his suffering, but she didn't know how to interpret, let alone address, his frustration after his admittance. Isabel exhaled loudly and she finally reached out and took his hand in hers. He squeezed it lightly. They stayed like that for a few seconds and then Isabel attempted to let him go.

'No, not yet,' David said, and Isabel could have sworn she heard the hint of desperation in his tone.

'David, what is it that you want from me? It is clear you are not interested in me so what is it that you are seeking? Is it my friendship?' Isabel asked, trying to keep calm though deep inside every word felt like a knife pricking her heart. David looked straight at her.

'Not interested in you? Seriously Isabel? Can't you see? I am in love with you. I have never met a woman who makes me feel the way you do.'

Isabel was stunned. 'Then why? Why can't we be together?' Isabel asked desperately. Was her aunt right. Was this man hiding a secret?

David breathed deeply. 'I am a sworn traveller, Isabel. I have made plans to travel to the edge of earth, see and experience the oddities of our world. I may be away for months. How can I ask my wife to tolerate my long absences?'

'I would never stay behind. I would travel with you.'

'Impossible! More than often, I find myself in life-threatening situations. Or I may go days without a proper meal and bath. How can I ask you to endure all that?'

'Is it because you think women can't withstand hardship?' Isabel asked feeling hurt that the man she loved didn't recognise her strength.

'You may be able to Isabel. I have never met anyone like you. Why do you think I am here with you? I want you to be my wife desperately,' David said and for the first time he leaned towards Isabel with his face so close to hers she could feel his breath on her cheek. Isabel's body tickled all over. He was going to kiss her. And he did. Right there, in the shaded thicket of Hyde Park, sitting on a blanket, in plain sight yet Isabel didn't care. She craved for this man, and she would never push him away even if it ruined her. His lips brushed hers, lightly, sensually. Isabel whimpered at the sensation. And, then, he grabbed her by the nape, and he deepened his kiss with urgency and desperation. His tongue searched for hers and Isabel felt fire burning every part of her.

She soon forgot where she was. She straddled him and let her breasts press against his torso. And she was ready to get bolder with her hand caressing his chest moving slowly south, but David lifted her from him and moved abruptly away from her. Isabel was desperate, with her swollen lips wanting more. David looked discomforted as well with a huge bulge in his trousers. He wanted her and Isabel grinned, blissful and hopeful.

'Dear Lord!' he exclaimed 'I tried so hard not to kiss you, woman, because I knew what it would do to me.'

Isabel looked at him in wonderment. She thought their kiss was divine. She could still taste him, smell his sandalwood perfume infused in her skin. She reached to touch him, but he moved even further away across the blanket, making her feel sick in the stomach. She now wanted to cry. How could he be so harsh?

'Why…? Why are you resisting this?' Isabel asked and then her aunt's words came to her again. 'Are you running away from something?'

David turned rapidly to face her and for the first time his eyes were not filled with ease and confidence. There was a dark shadow, unseen before. He tightened his lips in a thin line. Isabel was spooked. She stood up to leave but he grabbed her by the wrist, preventing her untimely departure.

'Who told you…?' He thundered. Isabel made to escape his grip, but he wouldn't let go.

'Tell me what?' she shouted boldly. 'David! Let me go at once!' she bellowed, and tears ran down her cheeks. At the sight of her crying, David's mien relaxed. He let her go and dropped his head in abandonment.

'I am sorry Isabel. I beg you to forgive me. Please don't

leave. Let me explain first.'

Isabel wanted to turn her back and run. She didn't like the sight of the broken man tucked sitting like a little boy in front of her. David had a secret, and she knew instinctively it was dark. Did she want to know? Her brain told her otherwise, but her heart told her something different; she couldn't abandon him. She reach out and let her fingers run through his hair. David relaxed his shoulders.

'You are right. I am running away. I am running away from the memories of my painful, despicable childhood. I am running away from a cruel father. A father that I hate. Every time I am in London, the idea of breathing the same air as this man makes me sick. I hardly ever stay in London but meeting you, talking to you, spending this time together makes this city tolerable, or even pleasant I would say. My instincts are telling me that it is time to go but my heart, the love I feel for you, keeps me here.'

Isabel's heart bloomed with happiness. David loved her and he found comfort in her. She immediately fell on her knees and hugged him. Moments passed and he relaxed, his body leaning into the contours of her curves, into her embrace.

'We can go and live anywhere in England or in the world, my love,' she whispered and gave him a little peck on his head. 'And if money is the issue, I have got plenty. My father has secured my independence.'

David roared with laughter. He put his arms around her and slid her onto his lap. He kissed her passionately running his hands all over her body. Isabel wanted to rip her gown off, to shred it, just to feel his touch on her bare skin but she soon remembered how exposed they were. She was certain she had made a spectacle of herself already and gossips would be severe upon her. She thought of her parents and the promise she had made to her Mother. She came to her senses immediately and pulled herself away from him and checked their surroundings. Nobody seemed to be lurking or strolling by, but she couldn't be certain.

'You love me too,' David stated matter-of-factly.

'I do,' Isabel answered with no hesitation whatsoever. 'But we need to make a decision, David. I am sorry to pressure you, but I can't risk my family's reputation. Not after what happened with the duke.'

'Do you realise the sacrifice you need to make, Isabel? We can't stay in London. Not until my father dies. He is old but virile from what I hear. I don't believe his demise is going to happen any time soon. You and your family will be apart.'

'But we will visit for a few days. Won't we?'

'Yes, we will,' David said and caressed Isabel's cheek. Isabel savoured the sensation, and she knew that it was a big price to pay to be with him but equally was certain he was worth it. Deep down she wanted to know what his father was like; what sort of a man could inspire such ill sentiment to his own flesh and blood? But David didn't seem keen in imparting any more details. Maybe in time she would find out but not today, not now. Now she sensed that her fate was taking the most unexpected and thrilling turn.

'And money, my love, is not an issue. I have got my own fortune,' he said and grinned at Isabel. Isabel smiled back, moved about her future prospects. She had finally found what she was dreaming about all along. A man of the world, well-educated, brave enough to face wild beasts and confess his feelings to the woman he loved. And more handsome than anyone she had ever met. Maybe the duke could be his match, but her David was free of society's conventions which she absolutely adored.

'And there is one more thing,' David said in a low, hesitant voice. He ran his hand across Isabel's braided hair. 'No children, Isabel. I do not wish to father any children.'

A bolt of lightning struck Isabel. Her face turned ashen, and she forgot to breathe. The story of Psyche and Eros invaded her thoughts. Absurd promises. Promises that may break a couple's commitment. And not having children was too much of a promise to make. She looked at David with teary eyes. She tried to talk but her voice was too weak. David closed his eyes.

'I see…' she said, and Isabel sat back on the blanket. She felt cold and lonely. Not baring children was too much of a sacrifice to make for any man. 'Why?' Isabel uttered in trembling voice.

'I hate the word *father*. How can I ever be one? How can I hear my children addressing me as such. I can love you as a husband. That I know for sure. But loving my children? I don't know…' he said.

The ride home, by David's side, was pure torment. Isabel just wanted to extinguish all memories of him. Why did fate have to be so cruel and bring this man to her path? She knew she was doomed as no other man would survive the comparison. She was simply destined to live a loveless life. The realisation pained her, and she felt the urge to turn to David, grab him by the lapel and scream at him. But when she faced him, her heart sunk. David was in pain. His eyes though steady on the road ahead, betrayed his desperation as did his trembling hands. Isabel's anger subsided and all she could think was how to comfort him. Her love. How could she make this better while she was in such pain herself? She took a deep breath and closed her eyes, praying to find the right words.

'David,' she whispered, and she lightly placed her hand on his trembling grip. 'Breathe, my love,' she said.

'Will you ever forgive me, Isabel?'

'There is nothing to forgive. Right now, it pains me to know we will live apart but one day…' Isabel had to stop. The words deprived her of air. She couldn't find the strength to go on.

'But one day…?' David asked desperately relying on Isabel to ease both their pain.

So, it fell on her to lie. Yes, she would lie, anything to offer David relief.

'One day we will realise that we made the right decision. That we were brave not to succumb to our desires and that our sensibility triumphed. I am certain that should we decide differently, we will end up suffering, or worse despise each other,' Isabel said and reverted her gaze from him. She knew well that their decision would haunt her forever. She had met the man of her dreams and then she had let him go. She felt defeated and a coward for not fighting for his love but how easy was it to fight against an enemy she was not aware of? *What was his demon?* Isabel wondered.

'I am such a coward,' David whispered and gripped ever tighter onto the reigns of his horse.

'If you are cowardly so am I,' Isabel offered. 'There must be something we can do David. I understand your fear of not feeling love about your children but let me remind you, you didn't expect to desire a wife either. It can happen. I am certain you will adore our children because it will be a testament of our love.'

David looked pensive and Isabel hoped she was actually making sense.

'And if you don't want our children to call you *father*, they can address you as papa, or Sir or pendulum for all that matters!'

'Pendulum?' David roared with laughter and Isabel's heart bloomed with happiness.

For the rest of the short journey, they stayed quiet, and Isabel felt that David was brooding over things. She was expecting his verdict, and she held her breath. When they reached Isabel's house David jumped hastily down his barouche and came to her aid. He offered his hand, but his hold was loose and lifeless. He hardly looked at her as she stood in front of him.

'Thank you, Miss Pearlbrooke. I wish you well in life.

Chapter 10

Not one tear. Isabel was stunned with herself. She felt pain and she missed David tremendously, but she couldn't bring herself to cry for the man. She hadn't seen him for days and she was certain that he had left London by now but somehow, she kept seeing him everywhere. Outside her bedroom window, a passerby would remind her of him. Or at the park when she was strolling with her mother and Lord Darren, she would look round only for David's image to appear and then disappear behind the trees a moment later. And at the theatre on Saturday, with Lord Sanders and her family. Isabel could have sworn she saw David among the crowds as she was walking across the foyer to their box but at closer inspection he was nowhere to be seen. She was starting to fear that she was actually losing her mind. She had to protect herself and her sanity and for that reason she vowed she wouldn't let herself collapse.

She was so determined to protect herself that she was actually started thinking the unthinkable. She was planning to get married. Yes! That was the solution to her problem. She was getting married for convenience and prospects. There was absolutely no reason for her to wait because she was certain she would never fall in love again. A marriage of convenience had worked to Catherine's advantage. Her friend seemed truly content. So why not her? Lord Sanders was a good man and seemed genuinely interested in her. They had stimulating conversations about art and politics. He was a good listener, and he didn't seem offended when Isabel was voicing her views. Adding to his virtues he was pleasing to the eye too. In fact, he was the most desirable bachelor of the season, and he wanted her. Isabel sighed with the thought. She should have been able to feel flattered, but she felt nothing.

Emptiness had nestled deep in her heart, but she was not upset. It was for the best. Tabula rasa. *What a blessing*, she thought. She was given the chance to start from zero and maybe form some friendship and companionship with her future husband. She had declared exactly that to Lord Sanders when he inquired what she aspired in a marriage. He claimed that he felt alike the night before at the ball of Lady Bickenlow. Like-mindedness was a good beginning Isabel thought, and she straightened her shoulders as she walked down the stairs to join her family for their breakfast.

On the landing, Esther, her lady's maid, rushed to her out of breath. She grabbed Isabel's both hands and jumped up and down excitingly.

'My lady, he is here!' she exclaimed, and her eyes shown with glee. 'He is with your father in the study. I am so happy. You are getting married,' she said grinning broadly.

Isabel took a deep breath and tried to match Esther's excitement but in vain. She tried to fake some contentment so as not to disappoint the poor woman who was obviously exhilarated. She forced herself to smile wide and hugged her in the hope of hiding her face giving herself time to compose.

'Exciting news,' Isabel managed to say but she felt nauseous. So, it was happening. Lord Sanders was there this very moment asking for her hand in marriage and for the first time tears filled her eyes.

'Tears of happiness! I knew it my lady. You two were meant to be,' Esther chirped.

Isabel forced herself to walk to the drawing room hoping that she would be alone. Her wish was granted, and she collapsed on the sofa. She covered her eyes that were now drowning in tears of misery and despair. How did Catherine do this? How could she live with the thought that the man she loved was out there but shared her bed with another? She had to ask her. She knew it was not the right thing to do but she needed her friend's guidance. *There must be a way to endure this*, Isabel thought and clenched her teeth.

'My lady, I am so sorry, but this is awkward...' Isabel dried her eyes quickly with her handkerchief and turned to look at the butler who was addressing her. Next to him stood Esther biting her lower lip.

'What is the matter?' Isabel whispered, still trying to resume her normal breathing and to stop sniffling.

'Lord Sanders is at the door asking to see you. He has flowers with him,' Esther explained.

'Lord Sanders?' Isabel asked quite confused. 'If Lord Sanders is at the door, then who is—?'

Isabel stood up abruptly. She ran past the two servants heading to her father's study. She didn't bother to knock. She burst into the room out of breath with a wisp of hope knowing it was enough to kill her if it were not true. Her eyes failed to adjust immediately to the sight in front of her. David was there. Sitting comfortably in an armchair right across from her father. As soon as David saw her, he stood up and smiled widely.

'Isabel, I was just…' he managed to say but he never finished his phrase. Isabel had already jumped into his arms and crushed her lips on his with passion and menace, wanting to punish the man for the torture he had subjected her to.

With her hand coiled around David's arm Isabel could not believe her luck. Her David was right beside her, walking in the garden of her house, talking to her, stealing kisses and making plans for their future union.

'I procured a special licence for our wedding as agreed. Are you sure, my love, you still want to rush ahead with our wedding? We could wait for a few more weeks until the banns are read out.'

'I am absolutely certain,' Isabel said. She wouldn't risk David's reverting discomfort that could make him change his mind. 'I have all I need for our wedding. I can't wait my love,' Isabel admitted excitedly.

David hugged her tightly and lifted her up the air. 'A couple more days and you will be finally mine,' he said

'I am yours.'

'I mean in my bed my love. I can't wait to make love to you.'

Isabel blushed profusely and she tingled all over. Secretly she felt restless too. At night she could hardly sleep, thinking about how David and she would become one. Yet she couldn't help wondering.

'David, I need to ask you. When a man and a woman come together, they may procreate. Does this mean you have changed your mind about us having children?' David let her slip gently back onto her feet as he dropped her to the ground, and they resumed their stroll. His silence made Isabel restless, but David did not seem bothered by her question.

'I have thought about it. I wouldn't have asked for your hand in marriage if I was not ready do give you children. But I need to ask you a precious favour. Can we wait until my father dies and I inherit my title? Then, I expect our life will be less volatile as I take up my duties and spend more time in London.'

Isabel was not a fool. She could see David's distaste when he described his future as an heir of an Earldom.

'That prospect doesn't make you happy,' Isabel offered.

'It doesn't,' David admitted. 'I asked my father to disown me as I want nothing of his and his legacy, but he refused. I think it's his way of punishing me forever but now with you at my side this prospect feels less irritating,' he said and smiled encouragingly to Isabel.

'Does this mean we will not consummate our marriage until your father dies?' Isabel blurted without giving it much thought.

'I am sorry?' David asked quite confused.

'I mean when a man beds a woman, there is a chance of conceiving,' Isabel pointed out raising both her eyebrows.

David chuckled. 'No, we don't have to wait. There are ways to prevent a pregnancy if we wish to,' David said, and he caressed Isabel's cheek.

'Good,' Isabel said. 'David, how are your climbing skills?'

'My climbing skills? I am quite competent I would say,' David answered intrigued.

'I have a clock in my room I would really like to show you,' Isabel said, and her cheeks turned rosy once again.

'You do?' David asked and smiled.

Isabel cleared her throat encouraged to continue by David's gentle caress of her arm.

'It's very special to me and I think you need to see it tonight. There is a tree right outside my window.'

'Yes, I know,' David admitted. 'I know exactly where your room is. All the time we spent apart, I used to walk by your house trying to get a glimpse of you.'

'So, I was not imagining you. I was certain you had fled London, and thought I was losing my mind,' Isabel confessed.

'I was following you around, I admit. Seeing you with suitors was unbearable. The thought of you in another man's arms made me sick to the very core. It was impossible to let you go.'

Isabel felt blissful hearing this.

'So, tonight are you coming?'

'How far are your parents' chambers from your bedroom?'

'Quite far. Why are you asking?'

'You will see or better yet, you will feel.'

Chapter 11

Isabel waited nervously by the window for David. She hoped nobody would catch sight of him. The scandal would be of unimaginable proportion. And her parents would be mortified if they knew what she was planning for the night. She had already made a complete fool of herself while having dinner with them. She kept smiling to herself and giggling uncontrollably for no obvious reason. Her parents looked on at her quite confused, but she couldn't help herself when she thought of the delicious touches and kisses to unspeakable places David had described vividly earlier that day.

And later, in her bedroom, while her maid was helping her to prepare for her sleep, she tortured the poor girl with her indecisiveness of what to wear and how to keep her hair for the night. Her lady's maid looked rather perplexed at first, but Isabel suspected that Esther realised her plan. She even warned her of the Bow Street runner that walked past their property in the course of the night. Isabel didn't pretend she didn't understand, and she thanked her for the warning. Esther had been her confidant all this time. Isabel knew well she would never betray her trust. An ally could be quite useful that night.

She should have been embarrassed but she was truly not. In a few minutes her future husband was climbing up a tree to sneak into her room to spend the night with her. But *what if he disappeared after the deed?* Isabel thought for a minute and her stomach tensed with worry. No, her David was an honest man, and he loved her. She was certain. He could never hurt her like that. Would he? She had to admit she didn't know much of the man she was about to follow to unknown and wild destinations far from the security of her family home. He hadn't even explained to her the reason he so despised his father. She then thought of Thalia and how long she tested her husband before she readily agreed to marrying him. She knew him inside out, but Isabel did not have the luxury to do so, nor would she be afforded the time to court any man for that long. She had to trust her instincts and her whole being was screaming that this man was her destiny. Good or bad it didn't matter. She knew deep in her soul that this man was meant to be in her life's path, love her, teach her, show her the world. She was craving for adventure in her life and only David could offer it to her.

She then heard the rustling sound of the leaves in the tree. She looked outside her window, but she couldn't see David just yet. However, she was certain he was coming to her. Her whole body was alerting her of his presence, as an electrifying wave of energy surged through her. She opened her window wider to facilitate his access and a cool breeze wafted past her and into the room. She shuddered against it. It was then that she noticed the light plinking of drizzle despite the bright moonlight that hadn't been yet obscured by the fast-moving clouds which scattered the darkening inky night sky. The leaves and the branches were visibly glowing, as if guiding the way for David, as if nature was conspiring to their union that evening. *The poor man will be drenched*, she thought but she knew well it would take a lot more than a little rain to deter him from coming to her.

She waited patiently while feeling her heart beating very fast. She finally saw him closing in. She moved back to give him space to climb in her room and when he did Isabel lost any sense of propriety and decorum. David stood right in front of her with a hint of a smile. Isabel couldn't stop gawking at her magnificent man as his white shirt, wet with the rain, was soaked against his sculpted torso. The depiction of Eros in the Louvre couldn't compare to his beauty. Isabel felt awe, and powerless, to think or move. She swallowed hard.

'Are you cold?' she managed to utter.

'Yes, a little. If you gave me something to dry off, it would be quite helpful,' he answered softly. Isabel immediately removed her robe and handed it to him. He gratefully accepted it. He slowly unbuttoned his shirt with one hand looking at Isabel intently but then his gaze left hers and ran the length of her body. Isabel then remembered that her night gown was quite translucent, but she didn't shy away. She noticed David's smile and slight nod, a clear sign of his approval.

He finished unbuttoning his shirt. It slipped to the floor. He then used Isabel's robe to dry his damp skin. The image of her garment touching David's naked body made her feel dizzy. She bit her lower lip as she wished it was her touching him. Was she allowed to do so? She imagined her lips kissing his body, worshiping him and her gown suddenly felt too restricting; her body and face burning.

'You are wicked, aren't you?' David said and chuckled. Isabel looked at him with her eyes wide open, betraying her horror. How could he know what she was contemplating? Was he a mind reader? She blushed profusely.

'I love wicked girls,' David said in a low sensual voice.

'How did you know?' Isabel muttered, with her head bowed, unable to face him.

He said nothing but let the back of his hand lightly caress her cheek. The gesture restored her nerves. She didn't want David to think she was a wanton, but this man made her feel inexplicable things. Her whole body was blossoming in his presence.

'Well?' he asked her.

Isabel was lost. What did he expect her to do?

'Well, what?' she asked.

'The clock?'

'Pardon me? What clock?' Isabel answered not having the slightest idea what David was referring to.

'You told me to come tonight to look at the special clock you keep in your chamber,' he answered quite serious.

Isabel was stunned. Did he really think that she invited him over for the clock? She looked at him with furrowed eyebrows betraying her wonder, but David seemed quite determined. Isabel turned round slowly and led the way.

'This is it,' she said glancing at David who seemed to examine it slowly.

'Quite a piece, my love,' he commented. 'I love the curved hood and the silver-plated chapter ring,' he explained, moving even closer to observe the gilded details. 'Stunning,' he went on saying. Isabel now started to feel confused. *This can't be happening*, she thought. They are all alone in her room with a four-poster bed and this man was wasting their time admiring her clock.

'Well, you are very right to find this piece special. But I don't think we can take it with us onboard. We are certain to encounter some rough seas, and I am afraid this precious heirloom may not make it to our end destination,' he said and patted Isabel's shoulder for comfort. Isabel stood still unable to fathom the situation.

'Right, I should probably take my leave now,' she heard him saying while moving towards the window.

'David, wait! Are you really leaving?'

'I think I should, my love. What do you think?' David answered and the glee in his eyes didn't escape Isabel's attention.

'But I thought we would…' Isabel began saying but she halted. What was she doing? Was she actually going to make inappropriate advances towards a man? She had lost her wits and David was the reason.

'What did you think, Isabel? That I would undress you…' he whispered, his fingers brushing the straps of the gown over her shoulders, exposing her bare body as the garment slipped to her feet. 'Or that I would probably do this to you?' he said as he let his thumb run over her nipple that hardened to his touch. Isabel started breathing faster, her whole body was aching for his touch. 'Dear Lord! You are just perfect,' he murmured and put Isabel in his strong embrace. He lifted her up with a quick move that made Isabel chuckle and pushed her back onto her bed.

He started unbuttoning his breeches. Isabel just looked at him in awe and when he freed his strong, proud manhood she lost her breath. Her man was perfect. She couldn't wait any longer. The longing was becoming unbearable.

He lay next to her and let his hand caress her throat, her chest, her tummy.

'Isabel, do you know what is going to happen?'

'I do. Thalia, my aunt, explained everything to me in much detail. I know that for the first time, I will feel some pain, but I am not afraid,' Isabel reassured David.

'No, you wouldn't be. And my love, I will make you so wet you will beg me to enter you,' he whispered in her ear and nipped her earlobe. He, then, ran his lips along her throat and moved lower. He got hold of both her breasts, squeezed them together and with his tongue teased both her nipples. Tingles spread all over Isabel's body and she felt her most sensitive spot awaken, wet, craving for attention. And when he drew her nipples hard in his mouth, Isabel couldn't handle it anymore.

'David! Please!' but she had no idea what she was pleading for.

David moved his hand lower then and he covered her womanhood. He palmed it and squeezed hard.

'You are mine. This is mine. Open your legs for me,' he commanded and then he moved south, his head between her legs. He lightly parted her sensitive folds and ran his tongue over her bud.

Isabel wanted to scream with pleasure. She bit her hand to beat the desire.

David wouldn't stop. He worked with his mouth while slowly he slipped his finger inside her.

'Yes! Isabel finally exclaimed, lost in a haze of lust. Her pleasure peaked and her pelvis tightened. Isabel felt her release surging through her body, blissful and exhilarated. She opened her eyes to find David looking at her smiling.

'You are so beautiful,' he murmured and moved closer

to kiss her. 'Did you enjoy this, my love?'

'It was divine. I never thought such pleasure existed. Do all men do this all the time?' she asked, and David chuckled.

'Not everybody cares to please their spouse, unfortunately. There are married women who never once experience what you just did.'

'This is too sad,' Isabel sighed. 'How about you? Did you enjoy it?' Isabel asked quite worried.

'Immensely,' David reassured her, 'but I haven't found my release yet. I am so hard right now, I could burst.'

'What can I do?' Isabel asked.

'I will teach you everything but right now you need to open your legs wide for me.'

Isabel did so and David moved his erection to her entrance. He slowly pushed inside allowing her time to adjust to his size with his gaze never leaving hers.

'Gosh, you are so tight,' he whispered.

'Is this bad?'

'No, I love it. It excites me. You excite me no end...' David then pushed hard inside her. Isabel felt a sting and for a minute she lost her breath. David again stopped. He caressed her hair, kissed her forehead, offering her comfort and easing the pain away.

'You and I are married now. You are my woman. I love you,' David whispered in her ear. Isabel was moved deeply by David's heartfelt admission. Tears filled her eyes.

'I will love you forever,' she said.

David then started moving, slowly retriggering the lustful sensation inside her that Isabel had experienced only minutes before.

'Yes, David! Faster, please.' And he obeyed her, going

faster, deeper, harder until Isabel started to feel her own pleasure building around him.

'David!' she exclaimed and tightened her grip to his shoulders.

"Yes, Isabel find your release now,' he uttered through his own battle to hold on for her.

And she did just as soon as David moved away to find his.

They hugged each other tightly. David stroked her hair and pecked her forehead and nose expressing his love and gratitude. Her happiness had reached unimaginable heights. Thank goodness, David had come to his senses and hadn't abandoned her. The thought of allowing any other man to touch her the way David did that night made her feel sick in her stomach. And she could feel only gratitude for her parents who gave their blessing to this union, knowing that this man was taking their only child away from them to foreign lands. Her mind unwillingly travelled to Catherine who right this moment was probably lying next to a man she didn't love. *Poor Catherine*, she thought as she fell asleep.

Chapter 12

Away from home…

October 1829

Dear Thalia,

I have so much to tell you. I am writing to you from Egypt. We are all well in our health and I am happy to report that I am deliriously happy on my adventures.

We reached the port of Alexandria two weeks ago. We stayed onboard for four weeks which was quite a feat. We decided to stay here to explore the most exquisite sights my eyes have ever beheld. How I longed you were here with me. The pyramids and the Sphynx took my breath away. You would have loved them. My David even arranged for us to go inside a pyramid and visit a secret crypt that only a selected few have ever had access to. I must admit, I was shaking with fear as we moved through the narrow, dimly lit corridors. The air was stuffy, and I was afraid that we would run out of oxygen but then I noticed a sweet, unearthly smell that made me feel such bliss.

Our guide pushed against a wall which magically opened wide revealing a small room behind it. The air was quite crisp, and my eyes took a few minutes to adjust to the near darkness but then I was mesmerised by the most unique treasures covering the floor. We were allowed to touch and admire the golden jewels, crowns and artefacts ornate with the most precious stones. But all these came with a sad story. We were standing at the tomb of a young prince. He hadn't reached his seven years when he expired and his parents, devastated, built a whole pyramid in his honour. I think my emotions took over me and started feeling quite dizzy and sick to my stomach. David had to carry me out. Don't be alarmed my dearest aunt. I felt like myself the minute we stepped outside into the clear air.

David takes such a good care of me. I feel free by his side. While on board I confided in him that once I dreamed of walking barefoot on the deck of the ship wearing breeches. The very next morning, I found a pair of breeches on our bed and all my shoes had disappeared. At first, I thought David was jesting but he encouraged me to put the breeches on and go for a walk. I agreed only after he promised he would never leave my side. The size of the garment was perfect, but he never revealed how he acquired it in the middle of the ocean.

When we took our first steps on the deck, the whole crew and the rest of the passengers were completely muted by the sight of me, but I honestly didn't care. I savoured the sensation of the varnished wood under my feet and the unrestricted movement and comfort of the male garment. I highly recommend you going for a walk in breeches at our precious Louvre though I must warn you; you will be met with some shocked looks and even faints of sensitive ladies! I felt so comfortable with my apparel that I resolved in wearing nothing else for the rest of our travel and I swear to you some of the female passengers followed my suit and thanked me for my ingeniousness.

I was struggling with this, but I can't keep it a secret from you, and I trust you will not reveal what I am about to impart to my parents. You almost lost me my dearest aunt. I never thought I would find myself in such a dangerous situation, but I guess it is part of the life I have chosen to lead. We were almost three weeks on our ship when the worst storm we had ever encountered broke. The gusts of winds were impossible for any human to walk against and the waves, my goodness, were washing over the ship's deck. We were instructed to stay in our cabins and with every hit and toss I thought it was the last we would endure before we sank. I was curled in my bed, praying and crying but David seemed completely at ease with the situation.

He was reassuring me that nothing wrong would befall us and his certainty kept me hoping. Until the screams of a distressed passenger alerted us both. David left our cabin to find out what was happening. I was scared that maybe the sea had started pouring in. David came back immediately to inform me that the youngest son of a family on board had left their cabin and ventured outside. Without giving it a second thought, David fastened a belt around his waist and rushed up the stairs. I followed him too in fear that he would do something thoughtless. I was surprised to hear him ordering the sailors to tie a rope to his belt and hold him tight as he passed the exit to the main deck. I never felt sicken in my life, the thought of losing my husband in that hell of a storm. And then the deafening sound of the broken mast ignited a fire in me and without a second thought I pushed past everybody and ran outside. The wind blew me over immediately and I felt my body rolling and bumping on hard objects like a lifeless doll unable to do anything. And when I thought my last breath was escaping my lungs, David was there to pull me up, holding me by one arm and the little boy in the other.

To this day, I don't understand how he managed us both. He brought us inside to safety and he ushered me to our cabin where *he dried me and held me tight in his strong embrace all night long. He didn't say anything to me after the incident. He could have scolded me for putting us all in danger. Instead, when I attempted to explain, he simply said he understood the feeling and that he forgave my recklessness as long as I promised to never do it again. He said that at least one of us should exhibit some sanity from time to time which made me laugh hard despite being shaken and bruised.*

David's heroic deed was quite celebrated on board. Everyone was talking about his courage and loved narrating the tale of David fighting the big waves and saving us with his inhuman power. The description progressively made him taller and more muscled than he already is. He lifted masts with his bare hands and fought whales by the time we reached port. I am pretty sure odes are recited to his honour describing him as this mythical creature who had more power than Hercules. I am so proud of him, but David is so humble. He never once boasted about his accomplishment. In fact, his life stories are full of heroism and more than once he has saved lives.

He dismissed the compliments sand any gestures of appreciation from the boy's family. The only appreciation he accepted was from the little boy himself, who hugged him tightly and the sight made my heart melt. David holding this young boy in his arms made me think of him holding and cuddling our own children in the future. He is going to be such a good father. I am certain. The thought, however, never crosses his mind. Whenever I try to bring the subject to his attention, he finds excuses to terminate our discussion. Childbearing is certainly not his desire, and it pains me, but I am hopeful that he will change his mind in the future. I will be patient.

In a couple of days, we are leaving Egypt and travelling to Bombay. We are sailing up the Nile thus no rough seas will be threatening us. David has a residence there which he thinks might be too small for the needs of a married couple, but I am confident we will find the house of our dreams very soon. And when we do, please promise you will come and visit.

Long to hear your news my dearest aunt. Please write back soon.

Yours sincerely,
Isabel

May 1830

Dear Thalia,

I must apologise for not writing sooner. I am so glad you are enjoying your travelling to Europe and your description of the museums you have visited made my heart flip with joy. I wish I could be there with you but travelling at present is not possible.

The last four months have been very busy with searching for a residence and organising a household for David and me. It turned out that the small residence he described was quite literal. The man lived in four walls with no staff. His possessions were a bed, two chairs and a table. Though I admire him for being able to live humbly with no need for material possessions, I cannot! We had to look for a new property and we managed to find the most beautiful house on the hilly outskirts of the city. The views are spectacular as we are surrounded by vast green lands and enjoy the cool breeze of the sea.

Our house is not as grand as my family home in London, but it is quite comfortable and bright. Every single window looks like a framed painting of the most glorious nature depiction we had so admired in Louvre. Our garden is full of deciduous and evergreen trees and the coloured foliage through the seasons makes me forget about the longing I feel for my homeland. I swear to you, the beauty brings me tears of joy or it could be just the fact that I am insanely in love with my husband. I wonder truly if my circumstance would make me equally happy if it wasn't for David.

David and I spend almost all day together

and the very few moments I find myself alone I admit I feel lonely, missing you, my friends and my family. Knowing that in a month or so David will have to resume travelling to conduct his trading business makes me desperate for some new friendships. Luckily, in the neighbouring property, resides a Spanish family, Mr and Mrs Castillas and their three children. Mr Castillas is the wealthiest tradesman here in Bombay and I have met his wife, Agnes, who is quite delightful. She called one morning while David had left home to go to town, and we had a very interesting talk. I suspect we can become very good friends as we both share a lot of common interests like reading romance novels and exploring. She promised she would show me some spectacular sites in the woods like a waterfall that we can swim in, and she will also teach me how to ride horses as most women here are quite skilled equestrians. I can't wait. I told David that I would like to host a dinner party to invite Mr and Mrs Castillas but my love says he does not want to spend an evening sharing my attention with people he doesn't know.

He is so in love with me and I with him. I am surprised I am not with child yet being intimate every day. Excuse my forwardness but I can't help fearing sometimes that I may have a problem, and I may not bear children. I know David is being very careful, but I can't see how he can always be mindful when lust takes over. I know I can't contain myself. Though this is such a bleak thought I know that such incapability would make David happy. Should I give up my aspiration of becoming a mother? I wonder.

Please visit us soon. I promise you, you will love Bombay. I believe that once you get here you will never want to leave. If you reach London, give a big hug to my parents on my behalf. I know they miss me tremendously though they don't complain in any of their letters. They always claim they are happy and of best health, but I can't help worrying.

Long to hear from you but I long to see you more.

Yours truly,
Isabel

December 1830

Dear Thalia,

How are you, my dearest? I miss you and your letters always bring me so much joy. Thank you for visiting my parents. Your account on their health and well-being gave me great relief. Here, life is quieter than I expected. To be honest, I never thought David's business would take him away for hours and hours. On the days he needs to ride to neighbouring towns or stay away for a few days, loneliness becomes unbearable. Luckily, I have Agnes to keep me company and we spend long mornings exploring the premises.

Our exploration one day took us to the town in the working-class neighbourhoods. I swear to you, Agnes and I were utterly shocked. People lived in horrible conditions. The houses were tiny and cramped. Everything looked dark and dirty, and the smell made me feel sick. Despite being abhorred, Agnes and I kept walking in the streets semi-disguised in the humblest of outfits we borrowed from our maids. The living conditions were subhuman. The only ray of sunshine were the children who played in the streets cheerfully, kicking rocks or fencing with sticks. Their clothes were torn, and they had no shoes on their feet but still they laughed and seemed happy. Then, a little girl reached out to us and asked for food which nearly broke my heart. Agnes and I decided that we needed to do something for these children. We returned home and we ordered some cakes, bread and some meat to be prepared. We also found some clothes for them. Of course, I didn't have any children's clothes, but Agnes is a mother of three and she had some used to give away to those poor children. When I explained our plan to David, he was very supportive though he was a little upset we had ventured all alone in that neighbourhood. He insisted on taking us in his barouche the next day and made me promise never to go back unless he was there or at least accompanied by one of the servants.

The next day, the gratitude and the cheers of the children filled my heart with happiness. I never felt so moved in my life. Some children were devouring the food, but I noticed some were not eating at all. Instead, they were hiding their food under their garments. When Agnes asked them in their native language the reason, they told us that they preferred taking the treats to their family who had been starving for days. Those children, though famished, put their families first. How noble is this? And then I noticed another girl who never came close to us but stood nearby with her hands crossed over her chest, looking quite angry. She couldn't have been more than nine and as I was approaching her, I noticed her eyes had the most striking golden colour that took my breath away. I offered her a loaf of bread which she refused to take, turning and looking away from me. I was really perplexed, and I called Agnes over to try and talk some sense into this girl. The girl surprised us both when, in impeccable English, she asked us if we were bringing them food every day. Agnes and I were rendered speechless gazing at her with our eyes wide open like two ninnies. We had no answer for her. She then laughed at us, and she said that she didn't want our food since the next day she was going to be hungry again and the memory of the freshly baked loaf would make her longing even worse. Her reasoning made sense, and we left her, feeling defeated. On our way back home, we started discussing the prospect of offering food more often to these forsaken children. We decided to have more families involved and luckily David agreed to our plan and promised to support us. Agnes and I organised gatherings with ladies in our community. We described to them the situation, and many agreed to help us. We collect money to buy food and clothing. We call ourselves the "Charming Saviours" which makes us all laugh. It's our little women's club. This activity has given me so much joy and purpose in life.

I have even started teaching that girl three times a week. Her name is Melia. Though resistant at first, I persuaded her that education is the single most important asset for her future prospects and luckily, she understood. She has made a remarkable progress in reading and writing. She is such a bright little girl. Imagine that she managed to learn English only by listening to sailors and the workers at the port where she and her mother sold flowers some days or helped her father with carrying baggage. I hope my own daughter will match her brightness and wit.

Our lessons take place outdoors, in a shed that her father built for us to sit. Her parents are the nicest people, their eyes betraying the gratitude they feel for my attention to their daughter. So far, the outdoor space works but during the rainy season, we will not be able to continue sitting outside and the family will never invite me inside their home. They are too ashamed I believe. I asked David if we could invite Melia to stay with us during that period. It would have helped her excel so much in her education and I will not have to travel in muddy roads that Melia explained sometimes get flooded. David was not happy with the prospect, but I think I can persuade him if I insist. He complains sometimes that my charity work is time consuming. He is feeling neglected, but I cannot give it up. I am blissful knowing that I make a difference to the lives of the most unfortunate. I hate to disappoint my husband, but I am trying my best to please him, and, on most occasions, I think he is content.

There is one more thing that I would like to confess to you, Thalia. There is a little something that I observed with David that worries me a lot. I am starting to fear that his adventurous stories and the dangers he bravely faced were not random occurrences. I am starting to think that he may be voluntarily finding himself in unfortunate and dangerous situations. I noticed that he is always the very first to respond to distress such as putting out fires or any other disaster. He returns to me with a bruised face and a limp, describing situations where he had to fight highway men who attacked wealthy innocents or got in the middle of a fist fight to protect the weak. Last week, he came back home badly wounded by a knife! The story was that he witnessed a thief threatening a family in the street. He happened to ride by and when he noticed the commotion he jumped off his horse and fought the criminal with bare hands. He managed to scare him off but not before he got injured. Luckily the wound was not deep, and he healed quickly. I am so scared when he leaves home and travels knowing with certainty, he will come back with a story of near death. I know I should feel proud of him being courageous and defending the weak, but I can't see why he has to do this all alone and without asking for our servants help. Or why he doesn't call for the constabulary. Not all situations require his involvement I am certain. I begged him to be more careful and I explained my fears. I told him that losing him would be the end of me, but I don't think I have convinced him. I am so afraid cousin. What should I do?

I hope I didn't make you sad. I assure you I am still perfectly content. Please write back soon with all the gossip and news of London and Paris. Your spicy accounts have made me the most popular among our charity club. All the women are holding their breath to find out what happened with Lady Barley who caught her husband cheating with her sister; and how

*about the daughter of Lord and Lady Folley?
Did they manage to track the poor girl who
went missing after her elopement with their
servant?*

Long to hear from you soon.

Yours truly,
Isabel

October 1831

Dear Thalia,

*The tidings are not good. I am a broken
woman, if I can call myself that anymore.
I had a son, and I lost him. I am hurting so
much.*

*Five months ago, I found out I was with
child. I didn't realise at first. The signs were
all there, weakness, vomiting and dizziness
but I refused to acknowledge it. I had to be
certain because if that wasn't the case the
disappointment would have been unbearable.
David was the first to voice it. He noticed the
change in my body, and he asked about my
menses. When I told him that I missed them
last month, he paled immediately. He seemed
utterly shocked but his reaction, though
disheartening, confirmed my hope. I never
felt so blissful in my life. I started crying,
thanking our Lord for blessing us with such a*

gift. I was so lost in my thoughts that I didn't even notice David had left our chamber. When I found him, he seemed less upset, but he was far from happy. I asked him how I was with child, and he admitted he had lost control on two occasions. He also said that he was ready to accept the consequences of his recklessness. It was not how I hoped David would welcome the news, but he was doing his best and I could not blame him knowing how he despised the thought of becoming a father. But I was certain he would change his mind, when the time came to hold his own flesh and blood in his hands. I had so much faith in him once but now it's all gone...

David was slowly coming to terms with my condition until that cursed letter. It was from his family's lawyer. His father was dying, and he was requested to return to England. I was with him when he read the contents and, I swear to you, in that very moment my husband was lost forever. The man I saw in front of me was a stranger, with the darkest eyes. His mien was rigid, and I never once saw his smile again. I had lost him yet every day I hoped his spirit would return but alas. David didn't want to inherit his father's title and step into his role. I told him that we didn't have to go back, that I was perfectly content with our circumstances, but he was unmoved. He kept saying that his father had won, that he had once again trapped him with his death and what's worse, he was convinced that the foetus was tainted by his father evil spirit! His behaviour became erratic, and every night he left our home only to return early in the following morning with bruises, cuts and injuries that went deeper and became more serious as days passed by. I stopped asking him how he got hurt because I was certain no heroic deeds were the cause of his misfortune. He was killing himself and I knew it. But I tried to stay calm, begging him every day to talk to me, for the sake of our unborn child but he wouldn't relent. He showed me no favour and that hurt me immensely.

Then, one night he didn't return and nor the day after. I was worried sick. All his belongings were at home and his horses stabled so I knew he hadn't left town. I formed a small search group with my most trusted servants. I couldn't let anyone know that my husband was missing and had potentially lost his mind. I had no one to turn to, my dear aunt. No one to lean on. No one to confess the misfortune that had befallen our household. We left home, almost certain that we would discover him dead and abandoned at the side of a road. I was at the edge of insanity , feeling despair but I forced myself to stay strong because even if David was not alive, he lived within me. I had to protect our baby because he was David's gift to me.

It was dark when we decided to return home.

We were all exhausted and especially me. We had searched everywhere, all the town's streets and lanes, the outskirts, taverns and shady clubs and all manner of establishments. Our servants were vigilant and ready to protect me. They warned me against some of the areas that I insisted on visiting but they never refused me. They never left my side.

In our carriage ride back home, I was drifting off to sleep, feeling quite beaten. I don't remember much. I have no recollection of what happened, but I remember opening my eyes lying on the ceiling of my carriage. I remember trying to look around, but I couldn't turn, and it was pitch with night. I could hear only screams and moaning. I realised that we had had an accident and then the pain shot through my body. I knew I was badly hurt. I tried to reach my belly to cover it with my hands, hoping to protect my baby but it was impossible to move.

I don't know who rescued me and how I got home. All I know is that two voices woke me up. At first, I convinced myself I was having a nightmare but as I opened my eyes, I saw David and the doctor through my blurred vision. The doctor was telling him that the baby was gone and that he had been a perfectly developed boy. He also informed him that because of the amount of blood and the injury I sustained he thought it would be impossible to bare any more children. David smiled and patted the doctor's shoulder as if he was delivering him the best of news. Even the doctor was perplexed and repeated his assessment almost certain my husband hadn't understood him. David reassured him of the opposite.

Thalia, I will confess it to you because the emotion is coiling around my neck, squeezing it tight like an evil serpent, trying to choke me to death. I hate him! I can't look at him anymore without feeling disgusted. He tries hard to please me, and he does his best to help me recover but seeing him rejoice in the loss of our child drained any emotions I ever had for this man. I can't face him any more let alone allow him to touch me. I want to get away from him and he knows it. He is hurting. I can see that, but I can't change my feelings. I feel betrayed. If he hadn't disappeared, if I hadn't gone out searching for him, I would still have my baby boy growing inside me. He denies this fact. He says that I overreacted to his absence and when I asked him, he refused to reveal where he was. David tries to convince me that the accident was fate. The loss of our baby and me being barren gives him great relief and he assures me that he worships me. He accepts my deficiency and that is what should make me happy. My husband accepts me for who I am so why can't I forgive him? Maybe it's grief and if I give myself some time, I will be able to forget and love David again.

Right now, this seems impossible and all I can think of is how I can come back to you. I need to feel safe again and I don't think David can offer me this anymore.

I know I am giving you grief and I wish I had more joyous news to impart. I reassure you that I am getting stronger every day and soon I will be able to return to my charity duties. David is still resisting but eventually he will have to return to London. I will try to convince him too because this place is too grievous for me.

I will write back soon.
Sincerely Yours,
Isabel

January 1832

Dear Thalia,

I am coming home. David is no longer with us.

Yours truly,
Isabel

Chapter 13

London, 1835

Isabel leaned back and relaxed against the carriage seat. She closed her eyes and allowed herself to breathe deep. Her day, though exhausting, had been quite fruitful. Her dream of building a school for those children most impoverished was coming true at last. The old stable at Clerkenwell Close, now modified into an airy and pleasant establishment, was big enough to accommodate the needs of twenty children her contractor informed her.

The once run-down building now housed a spacious classroom with big windows, three sleeping dorms and a fully equipped kitchen. Isabel sighed audibly expressing her relief. Everything had gone well she had to admit but she had not been alone in bringing this project to fruition. She had the support of her friends, Catherine and Diana. And the biggest advocate proved to be Lydia, the Duchess of Rutland, who she could now call a friend without any doubt in her mind. From the first day back in London, broken and lost, the three women stood by her, giving her comfort and helping her find her footing again. Her parents offered their support too, but Isabel could see their pain. She was certain they blamed themselves for her misfortune having given their blessing to a wedding that proved disastrously unsuitable. But had it been really?

Isabel was hurt immensely because of her husband's cruel behaviour and erratic changes in personality, and she would likely never be able to fall in love again. But if it wasn't for David and their adventure, she wouldn't have found her purpose in life. Now, she knew it well. All her experiences had paved her way to giving comfort and helping the poor innocents.

Nothing made her happier than the smile of the young child, when offered a piece of freshly baked cake, or the pride she saw in them once they were able to read the printed words of a book. And now that she was aware of her destiny, she felt ready to forgive David and was finally able to look back at the time they spent together with a smile and warm nostalgia. Isabel let her mind drift to the happy times in Bombay, to her beautiful garden and her pleasant household. It was exactly what she was trying to replicate in her school. She wanted the poor children to feel safe and loved. To learn like her little student, Melia, had learnt, thirsty and hungry for words and knowledge.

Isabel flinched at Melia's memory. She had loved and cared deeply for the little girl and leaving her behind had been the toughest decision she ever made. She even contemplated adopting her, to promising her parents that she would offer their daughter a life of prospects and comfort, but she could not bring herself to ask them. Instead, Isabel arranged for her mother to work as a maid at the Castillas', and made Agnes promise her that she would take good care of the girl and personally oversee her studies. Isabel could still feel Melia's tight hug the day they were saying their farewells.

'My lady, are you well?' Isabel's thoughts were interrupted by the distressed voice of Esther, her loyal lady's maid who never left her side, not once, since Isabel's return. She watched her like a hawk making sure Isabel had everything she needed.

Isabel opened her eyes and looked at the woman. To her shame, it was the first time she was paying attention to Esther in three days. The poor thing looked exhausted; her eyes puffy with semi circles of dark beneath them, her face pale, no doubt due to sleep deprivation. For three days they hadn't left the school, putting everything in place and cleaning, trying to prepare the space for the newcomers in two days' time.

'My dearest Esther, you always worry about me. I am well but I am ashamed I didn't look after you all those days gone by,' Isabel said and reached out to caress the woman's cheek. 'You look exhausted.'

'I am fine,' she said, trying rather too obviously to stifle a yawn that watered her eyes. 'You were crying, my lady,' she stated.

'I was?' Isabel asked and touched her face to find it damp with tears. 'I didn't realise,' she admitted, and she could see Esther's feelings of sorrow for her. 'These are not tears of sadness,' she said. 'I am happy, Esther. Honestly, I am. Look how much we have accomplished these past few days. Our classroom is finally furnished; the linen is freshly washed, and the beds made. Our kitchen is fully stocked and ready for use. How can I not be deliriously happy?'

Finally, Esther nodded approvingly convinced that Isabel was telling the truth.

'However, Esther, I am worried about you. You have worked so hard lately, and I do believe you need to get some rest. Maybe you should join my parents in the countryside and spend some time there for some recuperation.'

Esther's eyes grew huge with horror. 'I can't leave you, my lady. I promised your parents that I would care for you while they are away.'

'I am not a young girl anymore.'

Esther bit down on her lower lip, clearly contemplating Isabel's proposal. 'No, there is no way I can leave you all alone,' Esther said decisively after a few minutes of silence.

'I am not alone. I have Catherine, Diana and Lydia who stand by me like true sisters. I have my school and soon my little students. And let us not forget Mrs Cabbage. We have been blessed with having her assist me to run the school. Thus, I am hardly alone. Don't you agree? I love having you around but these past three years you didn't once have a day's rest. I beg you, Esther. Go to my parents. And if I need anything I will write to you to come back. It's only a day's ride.'

Isabel could see Esther gradually relaxing and easing to the thought, though it made her nervous at having to manage the house without her help. However, she also craved for some privacy as Esther had become her shadow for far too long. Not that she had any ideas of what to do with her privateness really. She had no social life. Her outings were scarce and because of this no suitors were interested in her. Not that she needed any male attention at present. Her days were full of her charity work, but she did admit to herself that she missed a warm male presence lying next to her in bed. The naughty thought gave her shivers, and she was certain her cheeks were raging red, but Esther didn't seem to notice.

'I think I will accept your kind offer, my lady,' Esther said with a hint of excitement. 'I have complete faith in Mrs Cabbage's help,' she said and giggled at the same time. 'Only I want to be in the classroom when Mrs Cabbage introduces herself to our students. I am certain they will laugh heartily.'

Isabel shared Esther's mirth. Mrs Cabbage was such a kind-hearted lady, and she never took offence to the reaction her name provoked upon introduction. She even jested with herself saying: *I am Mrs Cabbage. Not Mrs Cauliflower. Do not be confused, please! I smell so much better.*

Mrs Cabbage was a precious find. She had already been offering lessons to children in Bethnal Green, one of the most deprived areas and she was both driven and committed to her charity work. When Isabel approached her a year earlier with her aspirations to establish a boarding school for the poor, Mrs Cabbage was not convinced immediately of the sincerity of her intentions. But for the last few months she had been Isabel's most devoted assistant, supporting Isabel every step of the way and the last few days they had spent, all three of them, day and night at the school. It was an excruciating task sorting the garments, household goods and chattels that Isabel had managed to collect through her afternoon tea gatherings with ladies of the ton.

Of course, she often asked for donations and luckily, she was rarely denied. However, she knew she had to be careful not to overstep the ladies' kindnesses. She had her personal fortune and David's inheritance was significant to cover the expenses of her school for many years to come but she had to be careful with her finances and make prudent choices. She, also, needed political support and more people to care for her vision which, now, was known to a selected few. If she wanted to accomplish any change, she had to be vocal, but she was not ready yet to socialise with the haute ton.

What she really wished for was a life in the countryside which seemed more fitting to her needs. Peace and quiet was all she wanted, and children of her own, she admitted to herself with a heavy heart, knowing that this was a hopeless dream.

Chapter 14

'I am so glad you are here ladies!' Isabel exclaimed enthusiastically as she moved into her drawing room and found Catherine, Diana and Lydia having tea. Isabel hurried to take her seat and began unfolding a piece of paper with a long list of things she needed for the school opening. 'I need your help with the following. Please listen carefully as we don't have much time,' Isabel instructed.

'AHEM,' Isabel heard but she didn't bother looking up. 'AHEM.' Isabel finally looked away from her list and her jaw dropped.

'Thalia? When did you get here?' Isabel asked quite confused.

'Two days ago.'

'Pardon? Why wasn't I notified?' Isabel asked.

'I did send you a few missives,' Thalia said and smiled sweetly at Isabel who still could not process the sight of her aunt in her drawing room.

'Now you see,' Catherine said to Thalia.

'I do. You were right,' Thalia answered. Isabel did not understand the meaning of their exchange.

'I am sorry. What is the matter? My God! Is it my parents?' Isabel asked in a trembling voice.

'No, my dear. Your parents are well. It is you we are worried about,' Thalia said looking Isabel straight in the eyes.

'Me?'

Catherine, Diana and Lydia stood up, took turns in giving a small farewell peck on Isabel's cheek and made their way to the door without saying anything else.

Isabel stayed in her armchair still and speechless. She felt like an anxious young girl who was expecting her punishment for a mischief she had committed.

'Am I in trouble?' Isabel asked in all innocence.

Thalia's response was stern. 'Yes.'

Isabel's eyes grew huge, and her throat dried up. What had she done, she wondered. What mischiefs had she committed that made Thalia come all the way to London from Paris to scold her?

Thalia's chortle filled the room. Isabel started to relax and felt immense joy listening to her aunt's unconstrained, thunderous laugher once again.

'How I missed this… I am so glad you are here, though I suspect the reason for your visit is not that of leisure,' Isabel said.

'Indeed, it is not. Catherine wrote to me to come, and I can plainly see why,' Thalia said as she examined Isabel. Isabel looked down at her dress and she noticed for the first time the big stains and the creased edges of the fabric. She unconsciously ran her hand over her hair to find it oily, her untidy mane an embarrassment.

'I know how I look,' Isabel tried apologetically to explain herself, 'but it is not usually the state I am in. I had so many chores to prepare the school for our little students who are coming in but two days.'

'Hmm,' Thalia mumbled looking worryingly at Isabel. 'Come, sit next to me, Niece.'

Niece! Isabel thought. She knew well that her aunt only called her that when she had something serious to discuss with her. She got up reluctantly, a lump blocking her throat. Isabel sat down on the settee next to her and the proximity made her feel conscious of her bodily smell that did not do her justice. She wiggled uncomfortably on her seat and tried to cover some of the stains on the skirt of her dress with her palms.

'Do not worry, Niece. I am not going to scold you about your appearance today,' Thalia said and smiled encouragingly. Isabel sighed with relief and her shoulders relaxed. 'I am really worried though about your social conduct.'

'My social conduct?' Isabel asked with amazement. Had a false rumour or untrue accusation reached her aunt? 'But I do not have any social life other than my charity tea gatherings,' Isabel protested.

'Exactly,' Thalia confirmed. 'Catherine informed me of your unwillingness to socialise and partake in any entertainment. She wrote to me that you only care about your charity work to the point that it has become very difficult to discuss anything else with you. You are so obsessed that you have stopped paying any attention to the people around you who are either bored or overworked,' Thalia said, giving Isabel little opportunity to defend herself.

Isabel took in her aunt's harsh words, and she realised, for the first time, her reality. Thalia was right. She reflected on her afternoon tea gatherings and how less and less ladies of the ton attended them, finding the most absurd excuses not to be present. And then, she thought of the bloodshot eyes of Esther, her maid, and her ashen face. The poor woman had been suffering from exhaustion for months before she had even noticed it and, what was worse, Esther couldn't wait to leave her too.

'Dear me! What have I done?' Isabel exclaimed and tears flooded her eyes. She fell into her aunt's open arms and cried uncontrollably. She did so for a long while and Thalia only stayed silent, caressing her tenderly, offering her comfort and sympathy, allowing Isabel to unburden herself.

'I haven't cried that much, well, ever.' Isabel admitted with a sniffle when she was finally able to detach herself from Thalia. 'Oh no! Look what I have done to your beautiful dress,' Isabel cried out, pointing at Thalia's stained sleeve and tear-drenched decolletage.

'Do not worry about it. What matters is for you to feel better. Do you?'

Isabel admitted feeling that she finally got rid of some of the tension that was ailing her.

'Isabel, now you need to listen to me carefully. You are one of the most beautiful, smart, accomplished women I have ever met in my life. I am so proud of you. Despite your misfortune, you have found a noble purpose in life, but your entire life, your entire being, cannot be consumed by this.

Isabel bowed her head. She wanted to protest but the reality was that ever since David's death, all she thought about was how to offer comfort to all the children who suffered so desperately from poverty.

'You are still so young. You deserve to enjoy life! Go to balls, to the theatre, to museums. Learn, explore and be happy. You have your friends and me to support you, and we want to see you thrive. Do you know what Diana told me? That these past three years they missed you more than the time you were away,' Thalia said and then paused her emotional speech waiting for Isabel to respond but Isabel was lost.

'Where do I start?' Isabel answered reluctantly.

'What do you miss the most?'

'My reading and the theatre.'

'So that's what we will do first. We are going to Hatchards and then I am taking you to the theatre. It is time, Niece. And who knows. Maybe, one day, you will be able to love again.'

'Love? Oh no, that is out of the question,' Isabel protested. 'Love is the last thing on earth I need. I miss the male touch and the intimacy, but sentiments are not what I am looking for.'

'I understand the feeling,' Thalia admitted. 'That is how I felt for many years after I lost my husband. I wanted to stay detached to avoid getting hurt again. But somehow, I found love, and I am so happy. Falling in love is gloriously, nurturing.'

'I remember but I also remember the crushing, soul shattering loss. And death was not the worst of it. The realisation that the man I adored was not who I thought he was, was devastating. Love can deceive you; it can mask flaws and follies. I was foolish to trust David,' Isabel said and her heart pumped rapidly with anxiety. No! Love was not an option in her life.

'You hardly knew David before you got engaged. And I understand that you had no choice back then. Matched couples are not expected to get to know each other.

Marriage mart is a gambling game. But your circumstances are quite different now. You don't have the pressure of social conventions anymore. Nobody expects you to get married and produce heirs for some Duke or Earl. You are free to choose, sample and taste,' Thalia said, and she smiled suggestively.

'Sample and taste? Are you suggesting I should beget myself a lover? Isabel asked quite shocked.

'Lovers,' Thalia boasted.

'Excuse me?'

'Why not? With your beauty you can have any man your heart desires. Eroticism is a force of life, of creativity. Think of all the artists we have long admired at the Louvre. Passion and love are always discerned even in the gloomiest of settings. You should also find passion in your life. It's imperative if you want to continue with your charity work and make a difference. Otherwise living will soon turn into an unbearable burden. Laugh, cry, feel, make love, live!' Thalia added passionately.

'I admit I am really tempted to take your advice, Thalia. However, I am not willing to risk my soul again. How can I have intercourse with a man and make sure I will not fall for him or he for me. I don't have the strength nor the time for any more drama in my life,' Isabel said, and she huffed exasperated.

'Contracts! You will make your lover sign a contract. You will set the rules of your conduct, the number of times you meet, the location, and the duration of the liaison. That is what I became used to doing with mine,' Thalia offered.

'I do not understand,' Isabel answered, confusion contorting her flushed features.

'Contracts make quite clear that you do not wish for any emotional entanglement. It's a reminder of the true nature of the conduct you wish to have with your lover. An experienced lover, who does not look for a wife is always a safe choice. And there are plenty of those, I assure you. I would suggest meeting with your lover twice a week for a period of six months the most. These were my terms and for many years I enjoyed the company of men without any hard feelings when we parted company,' Thalia explained.

'May I remind you that you had the same arrangement with your current husband?' Isabel said and she didn't miss Thalia's sweet smile and the sparkle in her eyes which reflected her contemplation of the man she had since married.

'In this case I was careless. Jonathan was an infamous rake and spending time with him was special. We were compatible not only in bed but intellectually as well. He intrigued me and because of that I was admittedly more lenient with him, and I often broke my own rules. The two visits became three and then became daily. I never sent him away. Only when our contract expired, and I told him that I couldn't see him anymore, which was painful for both of us. We did manage to stay away from each other for a few months. Jonathan was a sworn bachelor and, feeling quite vulnerable, he even decided to leave Paris for a while, but he couldn't forget about me, and I could not forget about him. Thus, by the time he returned, he had already decided that his bachelor days were over. The man really tried to win my trust and finally I was able to admit to myself that I was in love with him too.'

'Any regrets?' Isabel asked.

'None whatsoever. These past six years have been the best of my life. Oh, how I wish that for you too.'

Isabel mulled over all her aunt had shared with her and made her decision. Her friends and Aunt Thalia were right. She ought to enjoy life more and why not? She would allow a man into her busy life. But she would take all the precautions she needed not to fall in love again.

Chapter 15

Nathan Dunkan couldn't shake off a bubbling excitement all morning. He was not sure what this unexpected feeling was. It could have been a premonition that something special was going to happen. Or maybe it was just the late night following the histrionics of Lady Brower when he had announced that he intended to break their liaison. He liked the woman, but he sensed that she was becoming attached to him despite his expressed aversion to commitment especially at this time in his life.

He was finally getting noticed as a playwright and not just as an actor. His theatre was full every night and the reviews of his play were good. He was not a fool. He knew well that the better part of the audience were women who attended hoping to speak with him and maybe even likely lure him to their beds.

The reviews, in contrast, came from men who seemed to recognise his talent as a writer though many commented that there was something missing. *It wasn't a masterpiece just yet but quite close*, he thought and smiled to himself while looking at his reflection in the mirror, observing his overnight stubble. He debated aloud with himself as to whether he should risk saving it. Mr Thorns, his devoted butler and the only member of staff he had in his home, was old and his hands were not as steady as they once had been. However, Nathan was willing to risk his welfare rather that hurt Mr Thorns' feelings. He loved the man dearly.

After the demise of his parents at the tender age of ten years old, Mr Thorns took care of him along with his older sister, Carolina who was seventeen at the time. And despite inheriting his father's baronet in Witney, West Oxfordshire, he on the rarest of occasions had any involvement with the duties that came with the title.

From a very young age he had shown his love for the arts. He was an avid reader of literature. He loved music and dancing and very often he would convince his friends to perform for the residents of their small rural community. He would prepare everything from the script to the costumes and props and the seating arrangements. It was the only game that excited him, and he had no interest for anything else. His sister always supported his peculiar pastime and never once complained about having to assume all the responsibilities of the household and the baronet.

Nathan considered himself lucky for his dutiful sister and when he received news while away in Cambridge, that she had fallen in love with their estate manager, Mr Furrell, he celebrated his immense luck. The man indeed lacked a title, but he was the most capable and trustworthy for managing his family's vast acreage. If his sister and he were to be married, he would be free to pursue his passion, knowing that these two had only his best of interests at heart.

He rode with speed back to her to give his blessing in

person. He attended his sister's haste wedding without questioning the couple's sudden decision; and a few days later he announced his intention to quit his studies and move to London to become an actor. Luckily, his sister didn't object, so he packed up his belongings and set to live in the family's house in Mayfair. Mr Thorns followed him obviously concerned for the young man's recklessness, obliged to keep an eye on him which gave comfort to young Nathan at the time. Their house, though located in a well sought area, was poorly furnished but it sufficed for the two men living alone.

The master bedroom and the study were the only two rooms his mother had redecorated before her demise and Nathan fell instantly in love with the place knowing that every piece of furniture and ornament had been hand-picked by his mother who he truly adored. There was no bedroom for Mr Thorns, but he decided upon on a nice airy room which had the magnificent views of a green park though poorly furnished with a settee and a small desk. Mr Thorns was perfectly content with his chamber. However, Nathan would never allow him to live in such poor conditions and immediately ordered a bed and a closet to be made for him. He had the little room furnished in no time, making sure Mr Thorns was comfortable. And when satisfied that they had both settled he set out to pursue his dream.

In London, Nathan did not have the easiest time. In his early twenties people questioned his talent, though he refused and never once used his title or his wealth to ingratiate himself. He kept his identity a secret and tried hard, doing menial work at first such as cleaning the stage and helping the actors with their lines. He listened carefully and observed them, taking in everything he could to learn each aspect of theatre and acting.

As the years went by he felt more confident and started performing himself, first in lesser roles and soon taking the lead. His astonishing performances along with his striking handsomeness made him well-known to the audiences and among his colleagues. Over ten years, he established himself as one of the best actors of his generation. But Nathan had not fulfilled his dream yet. His real aspiration was to become a successful playwright. A million ideas tortured his brain only stopping once he wrote them down on a piece of paper.

He penned and reworked scenes, never satisfied. Until one day he felt ready. He had his first finished play titled "The Marching Feud" and there was nothing he desired more than to see it performed on stage. It was a story of friendship between two men, Nat and Al, who fought side by side in a battlefield. They formed a brotherly bond forged by the hardships of battle. Until they both fell in love for the same woman, Mary, and their friendship turned into a violent feud.

Though reluctant at first, Nathan found the courage and presented his play to a Mr Donahue, a well-known patron of the theatre who immediately embraced the opportunity with one term. Nathan had to play the lead which he was more than happy to accept. The memory of the premier always made Nathan smile. He remembered vividly his nervousness despite his years of experience on stage. He had performed and prayed at the same time for all to go well. It had been the most nerve-racking experience. At the point in the play where Nat and Mary revealed their plan to marry, the reaction of the audience overwhelmed him. Al, blinded by rage challenged his friend in a duel. The audience gasped and women nearly fainted to the sight of the life-like blood but in the end, and just as Al was ready to stab his sword in his friend's heart, he halted. Their friendship became stronger, and they were able to make amends. The night had been a success.

From that day on, winding queues of people formed outside the theatre waiting patiently to secure their entrance or have a glimpse of the protagonists. Nathan was thrilled but at the same time realised he had to be a lot more careful if he wanted to keep his identity a secret as more people and especially women began asking about him. There were nights, when sure he was being followed, he took detours home to make sure nobody discovered where he lived. He valued his privacy and, now more than ever, he wanted to be left alone to think and create. Spending time in his study, enjoying the herbal tea Mr Thorns prepared for him along with hot, freshly baked sweet rusks was his happiest and most creative hour. He had never met a woman who deserved to have his little ritual sacrificed for.

Stubble it is! he thought to himself and with light steps descended the long staircase to make his way to the theatre. He wanted to get there early, to regroup and rethink some of the scenes. *What was missing?* he pondered again but any attempt to recall failed miserably. It was impossible to concentrate as the beauty of the nature all around him was hard to miss. Everything blossomed and the birds' chirping relaxed and overjoyed him.

'Nearly spring,' he sighed audibly. *The time of courting and mating for all creatures,* he thought and reminded himself of his resolution for the year: he was emotionally unavailable, though he admitted he needed women in his life, and of course, had to stay focused on his work. Falling in love would be a disaster at a time like this he pondered, yet there was something in the air; something inexplicable that made his heart pound with excitement.

Chapter 16

'You are late, Alistair!' Nathan scolded his co-protagonist. 'What took you so long and why are you smiling like a ninny?'

Alistair seemingly unoffended by Nathan's insult, continued whispering a happy tune, looked at himself in the mirror, ambling while putting on his costume.

'What the hell is wrong with you?' Nathan asked again, seeing his friend unaffected by his slight.

'I am getting married,' Alistair announced with a broad smile, yet unable to face his friend.

Nathan was not surprised by the news. Almost every week Alistair announced his upcoming nuptial agreement with some nymph only to decide she was not the one. Nathan shook his head.

'I am serious this time,' Alistair insisted.

'And who is the lucky lady?'

'Her name is Isabel; Thalia's niece. She is an angel, and she has no idea who I am yet. We are meeting in the foyer after the show. Do you remember Thalia?'

'Of course I do. You were marrying her too if I recall correctly a few years ago,' Nathan mocked him.

'We weren't meant to be. But with Isabel I am certain

we are destined for each other. Only she is not aware of it,' Alistair boasted as he put on his tricorn, the last piece of his stage uniform. 'Now, how do I look?' he asked and for the first time he faced his friend.

'Divine,' Nathan answered with a smirk.

'You need to promise me, Nathan. You will not approach this woman,' Alistair asked pleadingly taking Nathan by surprise. Never had Alistair asked him to stay away from a woman. He was too proud to admit he considered him competition as far as the ladies were concerned. And usually there was no conflict; they had completely different tastes. Alistair preferred them young and cheery while Nathan liked them more mature and experienced. He couldn't stand the giggly females of Alistair's usual pick.

'I promise.'

Alistair was full of surprises that evening. His performance on stage was his best one yet. Nathan knew how talented his friend was and that was why Alistair had been the first person he approached to offer him the part of Al. He always performed well but that evening he exceeded himself and all Nathan's expectations. Obvious that he was trying to impress someone. Nathan was truly curious to see the woman who was inspiring his friend to outdo himself.

He had planned to leave immediately after the end of the show, to avoid socialising with the patrons and honoured guests who lingered in the foyer to meet and congratulate the cast. However, he couldn't help himself; he had to at least see who was responsible for the transformation of his friend.

He walked decisively through the corridors bidding goodbye in haste in fear he might miss the special woman. At the theatre's entrance men and women surrounded him with their enthusiastic congratulations. He tried to respond politely, craning his neck, to get a glimpse of the two women talking with Alistair.

From their attire it was obvious they were members of the haute ton. He recognised Thalia who he had met years back when she and Alistair were flirting together but the other female had her back turned to him but saw she was holding a book. Not a reticule or a shawl. *Why would a woman bring a book to the theatre?* he wondered.

As if she heard his thoughts she turned and looked directly at him. Nathan caught his breath. She was an unearthly creature with blonde hair, blue eyes and pink luscious lips. She nodded at him saying hello and he nodded back not sure she had even addressed him. And then she moved towards him; people opening a path before her. Nathan observed how she didn't seem to notice how people looked or reacted in her presence. She walked with intent and when she stood in front of him, she smiled sweetly and curtsied. Nathan couldn't move. He had promised his friend not to approach this woman but now she had sought him out. *I am not to blame!* He looked towards Alistair who luckily was still engaged in conversation with Thalia.

'Mr Dunkan! I am so pleased to meet you. I would like to congratulate you on your wonderful performance. Alistair informed me you are the playwright, and I was so much impressed. I have never met a playwright in person,' she told him in merriment and Nathan simply stood gawking at her.

'Mr Dunkan?' she repeated his name. Nathan shook his head.

'Excuse me, you are…?'

'Pardon me sir. My name is Isabel Pearlbrooke,' she answered with a smile.

'Ms Pearlbrooke. We haven't previously met, have we?' he asked embarrassed by his inability to stop staring at the woman as if he was a green boy.

'No, we haven't. I've not been to this theatre before I admit. It is lovely,' Isabel answered at ease, but Nathan could not match her breeziness. He was struck by her beauty and an inexplicable attraction to this female came over him. If it wasn't for his promise to his friend, he would be bombarding her with all the compliments and courting tricks he had used numerous times. But his instincts also warned him that this was no usual woman who would succumb to his eloquent but quite banal flirting. Isabel became anxious with him being taciturn and he noted how she turned to leave. Letting her go would have been the right thing to do but Nathan couldn't allow that just yet.

'Your book Ms Pearlbrooke,' he blurted in a hurry. She halted. He reached out and took it from her hand letting his fingers lightly caress hers. The sensation was electrifying, and he had to remind himself to breathe. She too was affected; her cheeks instantly turned rosy red, and he loved it.

'I was at Hatchards before we came here,' she admitted and lowered her eyes for a few seconds trying to recompose herself.

'Ah! Romeo and Juliet. A hymn on love. You are going to adore it,' Nathan exclaimed.

'I am not so sure. I read it many years ago and hated

it. Everybody still says how wonderful it is so I thought I should give it a second chance; see it in a different light, maybe,' Isabel explained.

Nathan was stunned. 'Why didn't you like it?' he asked genuinely intrigued.

'I believed at the time that Romeo was a fickle character who abandoned his fiancée, Rosaline, because he fell instantly in love with Juliet. That behaviour is reckless, and the characters lacked depth in my opinion,' Isabel commented.

'Love can make a man and a woman mad despite their virtues. I have seen beasts turning into tamed sheep, humbled by the grandiose feeling.'

'Perhaps, you are right. My experience though has taught me to be sober in the matters of the heart. However, I am willing to revisit this play. Maybe it will resonate differently with me at this time of my life, but I doubt it,' Isabel confessed, and her countenance was not that of ease anymore. It was obvious that this woman had been hurt in the past and Nathan felt the urge to put his arms around her, hold her close to his chest and comfort her.

'Do you always go to the theatre with a book in hand?' Nathan asked.

'I will be honest with you. I adore my aunt, but we have quite a different opinion on what we consider an interesting play. So, when she suggested coming here, I decided to bring this book with me in fear of finding myself bored,' Isabel admitted and giggled.

Nathan examined the book closely and to his satisfaction noted that it hadn't been opened.

'So, what did you think of my play, then,' he asked encouraged.

'I liked it. I understood the protagonists and their feelings exactly. You have done a wonderful job portraying their virtues, flaws and follies. I liked the duel too. But…' Isabel halted for a second reluctant to continue.

'But there was something missing, wasn't there,' Nathan offered.

'I am afraid that is my feeling too. But I can't really tell what,' Isabel said, and she gazed pensively at Nathan.

'Perhaps, you need to watch my play again. And I would love to know what you thought of Romeo and Juliet.'

'Are you inviting back, Mr Dunkan?'

'Yes, Ms Pearlbrooke. I would love to see you here again,' Nathan said, and he didn't regret it.

A whole week passed, and Isabel hadn't returned to the theatre. Nathan started to get restless. Isabel was very much to his liking, and it was the first time a woman had not responded immediately to his invitation. But Isabel seemed not like any other woman he had met. She was special and he knew it. She intrigued him. He craved to know what she thought of Romeo and Juliet and to discuss his play with her.

Maybe he could pay her a visit. Would it be supportable? *Probably not,* he shook his head. They hardly knew each other though the special connection with her could not be denied. Maybe Alistair knew if she was planning to come to the theatre again. *Why would Alistair know?* he questioned himself. If Alistair knew wouldn't that mean that he was acquainted with her in a more personal way? The thought unsettled him. Alistair said that he was planning to court her. What if he did so and had succeeded? Nathan fought the weight of anxiousness bearing heavily on him. Alistair had been very quiet lately about his conquests. In the past he would not shut up about the special ladies he bedded. What could be different this time? He had to know. Maybe the time to address this was not the ideal as they were preparing to get on stage, but he had to know.

'How are you, my friend?' Nathan asked Alistair casually.

Alistair stopped buttoning his shirt and looked at Nathan worryingly.

'Why are you asking? You have never asked me before.'

'I am sure you are mistaken,' Nathan protested.

'Not once,' Alistair insisted. 'What's the matter?'

'Nothing. I was wondering about your love life though. You haven't mentioned any special ladies of the marrying kind of late,' Nathan commented with a grin.

'Since when are you interested in my love affairs?' Alistair asked with an arched eyebrow.

'I am just curious,' Nathan replied casually.

'If you have to know, I am courting a special lady,' Alistair admitted, and Nathan noticed something different in his friend's demeanour. His face immediately lit up after the confession and what's more he was not willing to impart any more information.

'I see,' Nathan said. 'Is it anyone I know?'

'I think you have met her once.'

Nathan felt a knot in his throat. 'Are you courting Isabel?' he blurted out.

Alistair was surprised.

'Isabel? Thalia's niece? No, it's not her. A divine woman but not my type,' Alistair said and smiled cheekily to Nathan. 'Are you taken with her?'

'I like her but if you are planning to court her, I will not pursue her,' Nathan confessed.

'Do not fret my friend. I am not going to duel you over the woman. Besides, I am quite certain she is interested in you too.'

'Is she?' Nathan asked with lifted spirits. 'Why? What did she say?'

'Nothing specific but she seemed very impressed with your play and when she came to talk to you, Thalia bombarded me with questions about you.'

'What did you say?' Nathan asked worryingly.

'Don't worry. I sang your praises,' Alistair said and winked at him. 'So, are you seeing her soon?'

'I am not certain. I have invited her back to the theatre, but she hasn't returned yet. And I do not know anything about her. She might be married for all I know,' Nathan said, pouting.

'She is widowed. It's been three years since her husband's demise. She lived in Bombay at the time and since returning she is involved in charity work. This is all I managed to learn from her aunt.'

Nathan should have been celebrating. Isabel was a free woman. However, it was obvious she was hurt, and he had to think twice before making any advances on her. He was not ready to commit to anyone and didn't wish to cause her any more pain.

Chapter 17

Isabel closed her book. She had just finished reading Romeo and Juliet. She would have reached the end of the book earlier but with Thalia around and all the outings she imposed on her she didn't have much time to sit back and enjoy a quiet evening. She loved her aunt dearly but guiltily welcomed the relief of seeing her off.

Over ten days she had attended every ball and gathering, visited museums and called on friends she hadn't seen in ages. But despite her busy social life, she woke up early every morning to go to her school and help her little students settle into their new routine. She was exhausted but at the same time exhilarated, she had to admit. She had become acquainted with many new people and had the opportunity to talk more about her charity and luckily the promises of help had followed.

But thinking back now, there was not a single man she thought intriguing enough to liaise with. Her mind meandered back to Nathan Dunkan, the stunning actor and playwright; her body tensed at his memory. His piercing green eyes made her feel dizzy when he peered at her and his mouth was sinful. Adding to his virtues, his play was truly interesting, a proof that the man possessed a quality of mind.

The evening Isabel had met him she tossed and turned in her bed haunted by his image, of him touching her and doing other delicious things to her.

The play. An idea crossed her mind. *I know what's missing. I have to tell Nathan.* Isabel looked at the clock; the performance would be close to its end.

She didn't have time to make herself presentable if she wanted to find him and share her ingeniousness. She was in her *deshabillé negligé,* a simple white dressing gown with a silk emerald petticoat, her hair loose. She could have waited until the next day, but her idea left her discombobulated. She ran to her wardrobe and grabbed her long black cloak with a hood, a garment she despised. It reminded her of the bleak period when wandering the streets of Bombay, disguised, looking for her husband, but it would adequately cover her informal attire. She, also, took hold of Romeo and Juliet and after a quick search in her library she was able to retrieve Sophocles' Oedipus, a play that had impacted her immensely. She ordered her carriage to come around and set off to the theatre in a hurry. She reached the theatre at the exact minute the audience was exiting the premises. She waited for a few minutes before she entered the theatre's foyer, hoping that most guests would have left by now. She looked around in agony for Nathan.

Some of the cast members conversed with the last few lingering patrons but Isabel could not see Nathan nor Alistair. She waited a little while longer, still covered in her long black hooded cloak not daring to remove it. As time went on, she started doubting her judgement. *What was I thinking leaving to come here in such a state?* Her cover up only made the situation worse, as it attracted the attendees unwanted attention who curiously gawped at her. She had to move fast if she wanted to avoid ridiculing herself. She decided to approach the only cast member she recognised, the female actress that played the role of Mary and ask for her help.

'Nathan! There is a strange woman asking for you in the foyer,' Mary said.

'A strange woman?' Nathan wondered, arching an eyebrow.

'I am certain she came after the end of the show, and she is covered head to toe in a black hooded cloak. And what's more, she is holding two books. To be honest she is a scary creature.'

'Books?' Nathan got butterflies in his stomach. He stood up abruptly and rushed to the foyer. It must have been Isabel. *Who else would show up in the theatre with books?* he thought and grinned from ear to ear.

The figure of the hooded woman had attracted everyone's attention. The bystanders were looking intently, whispering and hypothesising about the identity of the mystery woman. Nathan could see Isabel rocking from side to side, facing the floor, a clear sign of her awkwardness. He was baffled by her choice to appear in such mysterious apparel, and he rushed to her side wanting to save her from the prying, curious eyes.

'Is your carriage outside?' he asked her in urgency and Isabel nodded. They moved hastily outside. Nathan turned back to see some onlookers exiting right after them.

'Drive!' Isabel ordered her coachman. They both plummeted onto the leather coach seats and sighed in relief.

'That was a poor choice on my behalf,' Isabel admitted. 'I left home in a hurry, not having time to properly dress but my apparel obviously caused a havoc. I wouldn't be surprised if I see my caricature in a scandal sheet in the days to come,' Isabel said, shaking her head in despair.

Nathan knew that Isabel was right.

'Could you please remove the hood now?' he asked. 'I need to make sure it is actually you and not a deranged person who is abducting me,' Nathan jested causing Isabel to giggle.

'Prepare to be dazzled,' she announced and lowered her hood.

Nathan was dazzled indeed. Her beauty took his breath away and seeing her hair loose only made him wish she removed her cloak entirely so he could see all of her.

'You are very beautiful,' he said.

'You are very handsome too.' She returned the compliment and her cheeks blushed pink, but she didn't avert her eyes away from his. She liked him and Nathan felt his body hot and stiff in places that he wouldn't like to admit to her just yet.

'I know what is missing from your play,' Isabel boasted. 'You need to die!'

Nathan's eyes grew huge.

'I know that many playwrights' fames only come after their demise, but I was hoping that I would be lucky enough to experience success while living.'

Isabel's hand flew to her mouth, and she chuckled.

'I meant your character, Nat. What makes Romeo and Juliet an acclaimed masterpiece? Do you think the audience would be moved if the two youths were allowed to celebrate their love and live happily? I doubt it. I feel that audiences crave dramatic endings because they can then appreciate their own life circumstances,' Isabel said now breathless.

Nathan saw the logic behind Isabel's view. She was right. His excitement started to peak and match Isabel's. His mind started working quickly. He took hold of the Shakespearean play and tried to skim quickly through it, but it was too dark to read the passages of interest.

'And I brought Oedipus for you. This staggering Greek tragedy moved me, witnessing the rise and fall of the man. The final monologue is…' Isabel said but she couldn't go on with her thoughts. Her eyes filled with tears as she stretched her hand to give the book to Nathan. Nathan took hold of the book and smiled with sympathy to Isabel. He could see her pain, certain that it was not the fictional characters' plight that tortured her soul and protectiveness for the woman in front of him surged through him.

How could anyone hurt this magnificent creature? he wondered, and he envisaged himself as a valiant knight fighting thieves, beasts and dragons to save her. He stood and moved to sit next to her. The change surprised Isabel but she didn't protest or push him away.

'Are you familiar with this Sophocles play?' Isabel asked reluctantly looking at Nathan shyly.

'I am,' Nathan replied in a soft voice, and he slowly tucked a loose tendril of her hair behind her ear. 'Your idea is ingenious, Isabel. Thank you. And now I am going to kiss you,' Nathan said but he didn't move. He waited for Isabel's approval. Isabel bit her lower lip, looked deep into Nathan's eyes. She smiled and gave a nod.

They touched their lips to each other's, softly at first, savouring the sensation as their kiss gradually became more intense, hungry. Nathan found it impossible to stop and he wished Isabel felt the same. And when her tongue found his, he lost his mind. He stopped abruptly, looked into her eyes to find them hypnotised. He leaned forward again wanting to taste her. He kissed her neck, and her sigh made him dizzy. He wanted her like a mad man.

Over her attire, he caressed her thigh first, moving higher to her waist, to her tummy. But the halt of the carriage made him pause. They had reached their destination, and a feeling of urgency took over Nathan. *Is she going to send me away?* he wondered and hoped she wouldn't. He stopped and looked at her and Isabel with her eyes closed, seemed engrossed in the sensation of their kiss. She then opened her eyes and looked at Nathan with wonderment.

'The carriage has stopped,' Nathan said.

'Would you like…?' Isabel started but she stopped, and her face turned red.

'To come inside? Like a madman,' Nathan responded hoping that Isabel would not turn him down.

Isabel took his hand in hers and stepped outside the carriage. She led the way into the house without looking at him once. They both walked briskly up the staircase and only stopped when the door of Isabel's chamber closed behind them.

Nathan was not able to wait. He needed to feel her warmth, taste her body. He pinned her against the door, her hands trapped over her head and kissed her deeply, hard, showing his longing. He undressed her, admiring his self-restrain because he wanted to rip her clothes apart. And Isabel's sweet moaning as she leaned into his body betrayed her desperation too.

When all the forsaken garments were on the floor,

Nathan stopped to admire his conquest. He took a step back to scan her body and what he saw brought him to his knees. Her golden hair fell, free over her shoulders, all the way to her waist; her pinked cheeks and shiny blue eyes peered at him pleadingly; her perky breasts and her hard nipples moved rhythmically to her heavy breathing; her perfect tummy and round thighs reminded him of Venus's depiction.

He thanked his luck. He positioned her leg over his shoulder. His little pecks on her inner thigh, moving slowly up, invoked Isabel's moaning of divine pleasure. All Nathan wanted was to witness this woman's peak. He tortured her with his soft kisses on her thighs, her tummy. And when she gripped his hair, he knew her patience had run out. He parted her nether lips and with his tongue he teased again and again her sensitive bud. Her panting and sweet moaning sent shivers down his spine. He knew well, he would soon be witnessing what he was longing for. Isabel held on tight to his shoulders and threw her head back crying out his name.

'Nathan!'

Never had the sound of his name given him such pleasure. Isabel fell into his arms with abandonment. Nathan picked her up and laid her on the bed. He quickly removed all his clothes and lay on top of her, between her tented legs. His strong manhood was craving for her warmth, but he was not done teasing her. He placed the tip of his penis in her and stood still. He peered at her rosy face and her swollen red lips which he wanted to bite. Isabel opened her eyes and looked back at him.

'Nathan?'

'What do you want Isabel?' Nathan asked her coyly.

Isabel bit her lower lip and smiled

'You. I want you, ' she whispered

'What do you need?' he asked her out of breath.

'I need you inside me,' she said, looking boldly at him.

Nathan raided her, plunging inside her with force again and again until he felt her building around him. And when she reached her peak, he moved away and reached his.

Sated, he pulled Isabel into his arms and kissed her tenderly on the forehead, cheeks, and mouth. Her body tasted so sweet, and her flowery scent reminded him of home. He had just met this woman, but he felt he had known her all his life. They talked for the rest of the night about his play and exchanged ideas. He noticed he was not in any hurry, as he had so often in past circumstances, to leave her bed. His eyelids were heavy, and he knew well that Morpheus, the god of sleep, was coming for him. He was certain he would find Isabel in his dreams too and let himself relax in her warmth. He slept holding her tight all night.

Chapter 18

At home, after a long and busy day at school, Isabel's bath was ready for her. She submerged into the bathtub and allowed herself to relax; the fragrance of salts mixed with finely ground lavender and a hint of rose petals soothed her. Nathan loved her fragrance which made Isabel happy. She wanted to please this man, as he was pleasing her. Isabel smiled at the thought of their passionate nights over the past fortnight. But what she particularly enjoyed were their heated conversations about art and books that titillated his wild imagination.

More often, she would wake up in the middle of the night to find him seated at her secretaire, under the candlelight, writing. This image of him naked with his broad shoulders and muscled, toned torso was the most erotic. Most times she would leave him alone with his inspiration but there were times she was unable to resist. She would get up, apologise to him and straddle him. She would have him hard and fast, satisfying her craving and she would return to bed perfectly content and at ease. Isabel thanked her good luck. Nathan Dunkan was the ideal man, and her heart fluttered at this thought.

The feeling of bliss nauseated Isabel. She opened her

eyes in horror. Was she falling for the man? No! She couldn't allow herself to surrender to the feeling. She got out of the bathtub in a hurry, put on her robe and in her chamber, she searched her drawers for the contract she had drafted with Thalia.

She knew Nathan would come to her soon, as he did every night, after his performance. She finally found the document and she held it tight against her chest sighing with relief. She sat at her secretaire and went through it again. The wording was strict, she thought, but any emotional notes would have otherwise tampered with its intent. She had to make sure Nathan understood her stance on matters of the heart. Falling in love was not an option.

But what if the man was looking for a wife? Men wouldn't wed a barren woman nearing her third decade, Isabel thought. The realisation depressed but comforted her at the same time. What a peculiar feeling that was. Isabel shook her head and tried to concentrate on the document in front of her. *Visits?* Maybe three times a week?

Though she had enjoyed Nathan's daily visits over the last two weeks, she admitted waking tired in the mornings, not having adequate rest. She sometimes was unable to perform her daily tasks as efficiently as she would like. It was hard to do so when she were yawning every five seconds. Even Ms Cabbage worryingly enquired after her health the day before. She quickly jotted down *three days*. As for the duration of their liaison, she hoped Nathan would agree to six months. Thinking of the men she encountered on her outings, she was most at ease around Nathan, and he was definitely the handsomest and the most intriguing.

She then got to think about the most difficult part; one she had failed to discuss with her aunt. *How am I going to present him the document? What am I going to say?* Isabel started cudgelling her brain for the right words and at that moment she envied Nathan's talent of expressing his thoughts with such ease. Would he understand her? Maybe he would be perfectly happy with signing the contract without much explanation but if he found her proposal unreasonable, should she talk to him about her failed love matches? A failed engagement and a failed marriage were enough to justify her abhorrence to any romantic sentiments, weren't they?

The knock on the door interrupted her thoughts and before she even answered, Nathan barged in quite hyped. He didn't acknowledge her immediately. He walked towards her bed where with care he laid out some pieces of paper.

'You are the first to see this,' he boasted turning to her with a bright smile.

'What is it?' Isabel attempted to ask quite moved.

'I finished it,' Nathan said.

Isabel got up, careful to turn the contract face down. This was not the time to address the issue. It was a special time. Nathan trusted her with his amended script and all she could feel was honour and awe.

'May I?' she asked before she sat down on her bed and took the pages, holding them carefully as if she was caring for the most fragile and valuable object on earth. Nathan stood in the middle of the room and started performing.

'As I duel Al,' he said and extended his hand pretending to hold a sword, 'I give him a blow and hurt his arm. Imagine this Isabel... blood comes pouring from his body, the sight of which makes Nat realise his mistake. He falls on his knees to apologise, reaches out to comfort him and in that moment of weakness, Al strikes back and drives his sword deep into Nat's heart!' Nathan exclaimed dramatically and with his arms swinging, the contract on Isabel's secretaire fell to the floor. Isabel made her way to pick it up.

'I love it! The audience will be utterly shocked,' she commented gleefully, trying to get to the contract that had landed right in front of Nathan's spread legs.

'The play finishes with the dramatic monologue of Al who realises that his sinful deed is meant to torment him for his rest of his life,' Nathan added, and he stooped, his eyes falling instantly, and at the same time as Isabel's eyes, to the paper. 'What's this?' he asked. 'It has my name on it,' he said, intrigued, skimming through it.

'Nathan, stop! Please hand it to me. Now, is not the time,' Isabel asked pleadingly.

Nathan peered at Isabel and his mirth was gone. 'I don't understand. It looks like… is this a contract?' Nathan asked.

Isabel felt a knot in her throat. This was not how she wanted to have this discussion. She cleared her throat and tried to sound sober.

'It is not of importance, Nathan. Your play is what matters in this moment. I am so happy for you. Let's not discuss this any further today,' she pleaded.

'It says here that you want to see me three times a week,' Nathan said, his voice raised.

'I think it would be for the best. My schedule is quite demanding and seeing you every day for the last two weeks has taken its toll on me though I enjoyed every minute of it,' she added hurriedly.

Nathan squinted. 'In other words, Ms Pearlbrooke, I was a burden to you.'

'I never said that, Nathan!' Isabel exclaimed. 'Please try to understand.'

Nathan went on reading. 'Six months?' he chuckled. 'Never in my life, have I liaised with a woman for that long!' he said and looked at Isabel ironically.

'You can leave this arrangement any time you wish. This is only my proposal,' Isabel offered trying to sound calm and reasonable though as the words escaped her mouth, she knew well she was making no sense.

'Arrangement?' Nathan asked. 'What is this, Isabel?'

'I can't fall in love. I can't get hurt again!' Isabel hollered losing her equanimity. She was desperate to make him see. Tears welled behind her eyes. But Nathan stood still in front of her, unmoved, his eyebrows furrowed, his breathing becoming heavier.

'This is my way of protecting my heart. I need you to understand that for all the time we spend together, we can't become emotionally involved,' Isabel attempted to explain but Nathan shook his head with resentment. He threw the contract to the floor and left the room, the door banging on his way out.

How could she? he asked himself, hissing as he descended the stairs. Never in his life had a woman treated him this way.

'Nathan!' he heard her calling and he paused. *There. I knew she would come to her senses;* he thought certain she was running after him to apologise. He turned to face her with his arms crossed in front of his chest.

'You forgot your script,' she said, and she handed him

the document. She, then, turned her back on him and walked up the stairs. Nathan's jaw dropped unable to believe her indifference. He left her house, with his heart pumping fast and his jaw tight. *What a fool I was,* he thought and shook his head. All that time, he was certain Isabel had been enjoying his company and in reality, she couldn't wait to be rid of him. *But this can't be true.*

He halted his angry stomping for a second to compose and gather his thoughts. She said she loved the time they spend together and was definitely interested in continuing to see him, so what made him so upset? Nathan tried to understand his own resentment. It wasn't the six months' suggestion. *Was it?* It would have been unthinkable in the past but with Isabel the prospect didn't really feel like a burden. He resumed his stroll, this time much calmer and a clearer head.

If he wanted to be honest with himself, what really bothered him was her claim that she was not falling for him. She had wounded his pride. So many other women declared they were enamoured with him but not Isabel. *Why do you even care? You don't want to fall in love either.* Nathan shook his head. Maybe he had made a mistake. He should have stayed behind and listened to her. But still, he couldn't shake the nasty feeling of betrayal. Yes! Betrayal. That was the word he was looking for. He had trusted Isabel with his work, with his most intimate thoughts and she was not willing to trust him with her heart. Was that even a fair trade?

For many days after, Nathan searched for Isabel in the audience and lingered at the foyer after the end of the show a lot longer than usual hoping that she would come to him. But she never did. Nathan lost his sleep; he lost his peace of mind; he forgot his lines while performing; he was broken and all because of this woman. Alistair pleaded with him to share what tortured him, but Nathan was not willing to admit his defeat. But when he read a review that commented on his ill performance, Nathan made the decision to forget all about her. Ms Isabel Pearlbrooke was a bad influence.

Chapter 19

THE CONTEMPORARY DUNKAN MASTERPIECE. Isabel read the headline of the newspaper, and she beamed. Nathan's play was a huge success with the changes he had made, and Isabel couldn't help feeling as proud as a peacock knowing she had contributed. She missed Nathan tremendously and she craved to go to him but what could she really say to him? He had made it clear that he was not interested in a lasting affair. She remembered him sneering at the prospect of seeing her for six months. He had probably stayed as long as he had because of her good ideas and their discussions surrounding his play. He would most likely have left her after he had finished.

That was what Isabel had deduced by his unreasonable disappearance. *He was not interested in me at all,* Isabel thought as she entered the duke's residence to attend the annual ball that was considered the most anticipated event of the year.

The theme of the celebration was a well-guarded secret. Lydia refused to reveal it to anyone but as soon as Isabel stepped her foot inside the hall she could immediately tell. *Theatre!* Among the impressive flower arrangements, there were masks and theatrical props, and the servants were all dressed up as different characters, Romeo and Juliet, Othello, Frankenstein, they were all there. Isabel walked across the ballroom briskly, nodding and greeting acquaintances, searching for Lydia, Catherine and Diana. She found all three of them in the middle of the ballroom, talking. When they saw her, they grinned from ear to ear and whispered conspiratorially

'What are you three plotting?' Isabel asked, arching a brow.

'You can thank me later,' Lydia answered gleefully and they all stepped away to reveal their secret. Isabel's jaw dropped. It was Nathan! And he was surrounded by women; all fluttering their eyes at him.

'What is he doing here?' Isabel asked out of breath, feeling that her heart would escape her chest if it beat any harder.

'I invited him,' Lydia said proudly. 'I know actors are not ordinarily on the guest list but it was quite justified due to the theme and the success of Mr Dunkan's play. Wouldn't you agree?' Lydia asked, addressing Catherine and Diana.

'Absolutely,' Catherine boasted.

'Brilliant idea,' Diana offered and giggled.

'You are out of your mind!' Isabel said quite upset. 'What do you think you are going to accomplish with this scheme of yours?'

'Me? Nothing,' Lydia answered, looking at Isabel innocently. 'I just thought you would be happy to see him.'

'What gave you that idea?' Isabel asked with squinted eyes.

'The fact that you disguised yourself to go and see his play,' Catherine said, and Isabel instantly regretted she had confessed to them her act of desperation. She was dying to see Nathan perform their version of the play and she felt she wouldn't be welcome. Thus, she decided to put on plain clothes, cover her hair under a hat and wear her lady's maid's spectacles.

'I went to see his play, not him,' she protested knowing that her friends wouldn't be convinced.

'Well. He was eager to see you,' Lydia intoned coyly.

'He was? How do you know? Did you talk to him? Isabel asked.

'I was introduced to him last week in the theatre's foyer where he met John and I to pay his respects. I casually mentioned that we had heard about his play from our friend, Ms Pearlbrooke who highly recommended it. And it was the truth, was it not?'

Isabel covered her mouth with her hand and her eyes grew huge. 'It was but he did not have to know about it, did he?' Isabel scolded Lydia. 'So…' she continued.

'So…?' Lydia teased her.

'What did he say?' Isabel asked, blushing.

'I thought you didn't want to know.'

'I don't but…' Isabel tried to feign disinterest, but she was about to burst. 'Please tell me what he said.'

'Well, he enquired politely after your health, and he mentioned it was a great honour meeting you and…'

'And, and what else?' Isabel asked, biting her lower lip.

'I think that was it,' Lydia said, stroking her chin.

'That is hardly a desire to see me again,' Isabel commented and quite disappointed bowed her head.

'I think… he did mention… that he would like to see you again and that is why I extended our invitation to the ball today,' Lydia said with a bright smile.

Isabel wanted to kiss Lydia on hearing the news, but she managed to contain herself. She looked in Nathan's direction who, with all the women clamouring for his attention, was too busy to notice her.

'He is a very handsome man, and his manners are quite refined,' Lydia commented. 'I wouldn't be surprised if he had nobility ties. What do you know about him?' she asked Isabel.

Isabel got to thinking. She knew every inch of his body, but she had no idea who Nathan Dunkan really was.

'I only know that he is incredibly talented,' Isabel said and peered across at him.

At that very moment, their eyes met. They both smiled and nodded but none moved towards the other.

'Go to him,' Diana urged her. 'If you wait any longer there will be no dance left for you. Don't you see all these females waving their dance cards at him?'

'He looks rather pleased with himself. If he wants to talk to me, he has to approach me,' Isabel said and raised her chin. 'Besides I too am very busy tonight,' she said, and she intently displayed her dance card. It only took a few minutes for her card to fill, and Isabel looked at Nathan with a satisfied air; he did not seem that pleased with himself anymore. His mirth was gone but still he made no attempt to approach her.

For the entire night, they danced side by side. They didn't exchange one word; only glances and side looks. The intent of staying close to her was becoming too obvious in Isabel's mind but for the life of her she could not understand his stubbornness to stay quiet. Her dance card was full indeed, but she would gladly decline a partner if Nathan asked her to dance. For instance, Lord

Bright had signed her card twice and she had already had enough of him.

'So, Ms Pearlbrooke, you are a lover of the arts,' Lord Bright repeated and cleared his throat. 'I have to admit I am not familiar with any paintings or great literature, however, for women it is an acceptable pastime.'

Isabel tried hard not to roll her eyes at his comment and maintained her civility.

'I believe the arts is an acceptable pastime for any gender, my lord. Foraying into the arts, nourishes your soul, your mind. I would highly suggest you give it a try,' Isabel answered and smiled sweetly at the man who seemed enthralled by her.

'I am a pragmatist, Ms Pearlbrooke but if you were willing to teach me, I would be the most dedicated student.'

'Teach you, my lord? Isabel asked and raised an eyebrow.

'Yes, Ms Pearlbrooke. I have known you for a while now and I have been contemplating. Having a wife well educated and world travelled would be a great advantage for my unborn children and for myself. And you, Ms Pearlbrooke, I believe you meet the criteria I seek in a wife,' Lord Bright said and sighed. Isabel was stunned and for a few minutes she stared at the man speechless. She sensed his admiration but proposing marriage never crossed her mind.

'Lord Bright, I…'

'Do not rush with your answer, my lady. I know I may have shocked you, but I have wanted to reveal my intentions to you for a long time. This may not be the ideal circumstance and perhaps paying you a visit would have been more appropriate; however, my head and my heart say that you are the one I would like to wed.'

Lord Bright's confession was bold and honest. His eyes betrayed his longing and sincerity. And, as a man, he was pleasing to the eye. He was powerful, titled and well-liked. He had it all. Though flattered, Isabel could never consider his proposal or any proposal of marriage. He claimed he knew her, but he didn't know the most devasting fact about her. She could not give him any children and if he found out he would undoubtedly withdraw his offer of marriage. She was not ready to reveal this reality during a ball nor decline his offer on such a public occasion. The least she could do was to offer this man an explanation; and she would do so privately.

'Lord Bright, I am deeply honoured. Allow me some days to consider your offer, if you will.'

'Of course, Ms Pearlbrooke. I will soon pay you a visit. Would this be acceptable?'

'Yes, thank you,' Isabel said and smiled sweetly at the man .

Isabel made her way to Catherine and Diana feeling overwhelmed and somewhat dispirited.

'What happened?' Catherine asked worryingly.

'It's nothing. It will pass,' Isabel answered, unwilling to part with Lord Bright's proposal.

'Is it true?' Diana asked. 'Did Lord Bright just propose to you?'

'He did?' Catherine asked with amazement.

'Excuse me,' Isabel said and walked away. She needed a few moments alone. She exited the ballroom looking for some quietness. She followed a long corridor; she knew it would take her to the residence's library. Lydia was always very generous with her and invited her to skim through their impressive collection of books, so Isabel was aware of her way. When she entered the room, she closed the door behind her and leaned against it. She breathed in deeply and released the air from her lungs.

The news was out, and she didn't enjoy the attention. She wished Lord Bright had been more discreet in retrospect, but she could not blame the man. Other women would simply celebrate and boast about their conquest, however, Isabel felt sad and disliked the fact that she would have to disappoint the man and what is more, everyone would know about it. A reluctant knock on the door interrupted her thoughts.

'Isabel, may I come in?'

It was Nathan. *Dear God. If anyone saw him.* She quickly opened the door and pulled him in by the hand, locking the door behind him.

'This is unwise,' she commented but she could not be upset looking at Nathan. Being finally close to him filled her with happiness.

'Are you accepting his offer?' he asked with urgency.

'No, I am not going to accept. I am never getting married,' Isabel answered without hesitation.

Nathan exhaled with relief.

'Good,' he said and smiled wide.

'I would like to congratulate…'

'May I ask why?' Nathan interrupted her. 'Why are you so determined not to fall in love, have a family, children?'

'I had an accident, and I cannot have children,' Isabel admitted boldly. Nathan looked at her intently and Isabel admired his sober stance to her admittance. He didn't feel sorry for her, he didn't try to offer any comforting words. He just nodded.

'Thank you for trusting me with this,' he said and moved closer to her. He caressed her cheek. 'I missed you,' he said.

Isabel's heart flipped with joy. 'I missed you too,' she admitted and moved closer still, looking deep in his eyes. She longed for his kiss.

Nathan pulled her into his embrace, held her tight and kissed her hungrily. But suddenly he broke their kiss.

'I will sign your damn contract,' he said and nudged her nose with his.

'About the six months, you don't have to stay with me for that long. You can leave any time you desire,' Isabel said but Nathan didn't answer back. He just pecked her lips and smiled.

'Let's go home,' he said and Isabel, high on bliss, was no longer afraid.

Chapter 20

Nathan Dunkan, the sworn bachelor, was cheating. He always honoured his contracts but with the rules Isabel had suggested it was impossible to conform. For instance, to see her a mere three times a week was unfeasible. He craved her constantly. He would wake up in the middle of the night searching for her warm body next to his and if she wasn't there, he would simply be foul tempered all day. He couldn't imagine a day passing by without seeing her, touching her even fleetingly, stealing a kiss from her. After three months, he knew it well and there was no point in denying it any longer. He was completely and utterly enamoured with Ms Isabel Pearlbrooke.

In his desperation to see her more often he came up with a plan. He asked to visit her school. He toured the premises that were small indeed, but Isabel had managed to turn her school into a warm, welcoming household for those unbearably unfortunate children. He met her students, introduced himself, talked animatedly to them about his life's journey in the arts. The children enthusiastically bombarded him with questions about his play and his acting skills. Nathan demonstrated his skills to reenact different emotions from fear, to pain, from happiness, to confusion, all in a few minutes and engaged the children's imaginations. They tried to imitate his mannerisms through their facial expressions, arm gestures and postures. Some did remarkably well, and he offered them much encouragement and congratulations, but others lacked concentration and the confidence and, in the end, took the task less seriously making funny faces instead causing lots of laughter and merriment. And before he knew it, their discussion and the exercise turned into a role-play. The girls pretending to be fairies flying around the room waved their arms delicately and tiptoed across the wooden floors. The boys took on the role of valiant warriors fighting with invisible swords, their arms cutting through the air as they fought against invisible dragons and wild beasts. Nathan's enthusiasm and equally the children's was so great that he suggested teaching them drama and the students cheered to the prospect. Isabel had no other choice but to agree and she thanked him dearly.

Thus, Nathan Dunkan, the well-known actor and most talented playwright of his time, dragged himself out of bed very early in the morning. He grabbed a quick bite of Mr Thorns' freshly baked biscuits and made his merry way to Isabel's school at Clerkenwell Close which was quite a ride especially on rainy days. He felt cold most days and he was drenched to the bone by the time he reached his destination, but he didn't care. The warmth of the children's hugs and the glee in Isabel's eyes were enough to make him forget his misery.

He revelled in every minute he spent with his little students but most of all he savoured the chance to write a short play for them with Isabel's help. He cherished the moments they sat side by side, exchanging ideas and creating together. And every now and then he would taste her sweet lips. Luckily, Isabel didn't seem aware of how he truly felt about her. He was afraid that if she ever found out she would probably insist they stopped seeing each other. She more than once had expressed her fear of falling in love, but Nathan did not despair. He hoped that Isabel would change her mind, and she would eventually love him as much as he loved her. No one knew his secret apart from Mr Thorns. Though he never admitted it to him, Mr Thorns could see right through him.

'How was Ms Pearlbrooke, today?' he would ask Nathan when he returned home and Nathan was more than happy to describe his day with his students and sing his praises for the magnificent, considerate, selfless, tender, brilliant Ms Pearlbrooke.

'I would love to meet her one day,' Mr Thorns said every time. Nathan would offer him a thin smile knowing only too well that Isabel was never going to accept to make his acquaintance. That would be too intimate she would argue.

Alistair might have also suspected the truth especially after seeing Nathan digging about in the crampy and extremely dusty storage room looking for old props to use in his teaching and then, spending hours before and after his shows mending and polishing his finds. At first, Nathan appreciated Alistair's discretion observing him silently without making any teasing comments but then one day he could not help himself.

'When are you proposing to Ms Pearlbrooke?' he asked with a smirk.

Nathan's heart squeezed at the comment. He would have proposed to Isabel already if he believed she would accept but he knew better.

'Never,' he answered trying to sound indifferent, scrubbing with menace at an old crown that would be ideal in shape and size for the heads of young children.

'If you are not in love with the woman, why are you doing all this for her?' Alistair asked, scratching his head.

'I am doing this for the children of her school. They are all lovely. They deserve some happiness in their forlorn lives, and they have a great passion for the arts. This has nothing to do with her,' Nathan answered, trying to sound convincing.

Alistair shrugged and left and Nathan exhaled with relief. His feelings had to stay a secret.

Nathan is late, today, Isabel thought and kept walking back to the window hoping to see him approaching. The sun shone brightly, casting yellow light across the grey pavements, and the streets were quiet, thus she couldn't see what was keeping him away. And then, she saw him, turning the corner with his horse and her heart fluttered with excitement. This is how she felt every time she saw him, but she continued choosing to ignore it though it was becoming more difficult for her to push her growing feelings for him aside. She contemplated her feelings for Nathan Dunkan but dismissed the unsettling butterflies in her stomach immediately. She knew well there was no future for love in her life. Their contract had a finishing date, the 27th of July, when they would part their ways. She would love to call him a friend after that, but she knew it would be impossible to resist him and even worse to pretend she wouldn't care if she ever saw him with another woman. Thus, she had resolved to do everything in her power to avoid seeing Nathan ever again. But for now, she would simply enjoy his company as much as she could.

'Mr Dunkan is here!' she called out and she heard the hurried stomps in the corridor, the giggles and laughter of her young students as they made their way towards their little parlour where they had agreed to create a theatrical stage. By the time Nathan entered the front door they were all seated on the floor waiting silently and patiently for their favourite teacher. Isabel knew they wanted to make Nathan proud of them and they were always on their best behaviour. Isabel hurried to him and gave him a quick peck on the lips after making sure they were not being spied on.

'You were late today,' she whispered, and smiled sweetly at Nathan.

'Did you miss me?' he asked coyly.

'Of course I did,' she said and caressed his shoulder discretely.

'I missed you too. Tonight, I am going to show you just how much,' Nathan said and he winked at her. Isabel's cheeks instantly burned a rosy red, passion-filled desire filling her belly.

'Hush, Mr Dunkan. What if anyone hears you?' she pretended to scold him, but she was longing for their night together too.

Nathan started walking towards the parlour dragging a huge sack behind him.

'What is this?' Isabel asked all excited.

'Patience Ms Pearlbrooke, you will see,' he said and entered the room where he was greeted with an enthusiastic chorus of hellos from all children and hugs from the two youngest girls, Tina and Rosy. Isabel loved the sight of

Nathan among her students. He was so kind to them, and he genuinely seemed to enjoy their conversations and all the games they played together like blind man's buff and charades. *He will be a fantastic father to his own children,* Isabel thought, and her stomach tensed at the realisation that another woman will have the pleasure of giving this magnificent man children one day. Her eyes instantly filled with tears, and she cursed herself for not being able to contain her morose mood.

'Ms Pearlbrooke is crying!' little Rosy exclaimed and she hurried to Isabel, with her arms open in a hug. Isabel lifted her up and Rosy touched her cheeks with her little hands, caressing them lightly.

'Don't be sad, Ms Pearlbrooke,' she said.

To Isabel's mortification, all were now facing her, and Nathan dropped his sack with a loud bang and rushed to her side.

'Isabel?' he asked, his voice trembling revealing his immense worry. 'What's wrong? Are you in pain?' he asked and glanced over her body hurryingly looking to see if anything seemed out of place.

'I promise, it is nothing,' she said but she was unable to stop her tears from streaming down her cheeks. 'I'm sorry,' she said. She put down Rosy and rushed away wishing to find a quiet place to compose herself. *What a silly, silly woman I am!* she scolded herself, regretting her outburst. And what was worse, Nathan would not let the matter lie. She knew it well as he paced right behind her affording her no escape. She stopped and confronted him; he was indeed quite upset.

'What is wrong, Isabel? And please do not say nothing,' he pleaded.

Isabel exhaled, bowed her head and slumped her shoulders in defeat. She could not lie to Nathan.

'Seeing you surrounded by all these children makes my heart sing. It is such a happy sight,' she said and smiled thinly avoiding looking at Nathan. But Nathan didn't move. She knew her explanation obviously did not give him any peace. He waited patiently.

'A thought crossed my mind… that one day you will make a wonderful father while I will never…' she said, and she paused unable to continue.

Nathan pulled her into his arms and held her tightly. He kissed her hair, his breath warming her neck, creating the very feelings she wanted to deny to well up in her all over again.

'Isabel, listen to me carefully. Mothers are not only those women that birth children. What you do for these children is remarkable, sacred. You nourish and nurture them. These children adore you like a mother and more. Chin up Ms Pearlbrooke!' he said and with his index finger he tilted her face up to look at him. He kissed her eyes to dry them off. 'I lost my parents when I was very young, and I was lucky to have Mr Thorns who supported me like a true father. Though, I missed my biological parents I never felt unsafe or unloved. And all because of this man. I am so lucky to have him as are those children who are lucky to have you.'

Isabel smiled at him and leaned into him, squeezing him tight.

'Thank you, Nathan, you always have the right words. I would love to meet Mr Thorns one day. He must be a very special man,' she said, dabbing at her eyes with her lace handkerchief.

'He is. And he would love to meet you too,' Nathan said. 'Now let's go back to the parlour. I have a surprise for the children.'

When they walked back inside the parlour, most of the children were standing around the huge sack that Nathan had left abandoned in the middle of the otherwise empty room. Some children were observing it trying to make guesses about its content, while others were feeling the shapes through the fabric trying to make out the individual objects inside. In vain, Mrs Cabbage was trying to make them sit on their bottoms. Their curiosity had taken over and they were restless.

'I am sure it has sweets, cakes and chocolates,' young Theo said who was endearingly the chubbiest and had the healthiest appetite of all. 'If you go closer you can smell them,' he said and he leaned forward, pushed out his nose and began sniffing over the sack. 'Cinnamon and… vanilla. Yes!' he said and licked his lips with excitement.

'Don't be silly,' five-year-old, Tina protested. 'The sack is too big. I am sure it has clothes and shoes, no doubt they will all be used. I am sure,' she said and huffed in a dramatic manner; her disappointment clear on her face.

'Tina, my dear, we should be grateful for all the items, used or otherwise, kind people are offering us,' Ms Cabbage reminded her with tenderness.

'I know Ms Cabbage. And I am grateful, but I only wish I had something that was only for me. Something nobody else had ever worn before,' she said and pouted.

'I know exactly what there is inside,' Jonathan, who was the most studious, boasted. 'It's books!' he exclaimed rubbing his palms with delight while the rest of the children booed at the prospect of having to spend more hours of their time reading.

'Your torture is over,' Nathan said as he walked to the middle of the room. He picked up the sack and slowly emptied its content onto the carpet. Golden coins, vases, fake flowers, sparkling jewellery, pewter plates and cups and colourful fabrics flowed out and scattered across the floor.

'We are rich!' young Nigel exclaimed and started jumping up and down.

'Not quite,' Nathan chuckled. 'These are all props, and we are going to use them for our play,' Nathan explained.

'Can we touch them?' Tina asked, all her excitement tumbling out.

'Of course you can,' Nathan said and stepped to the side to allow space for all the children to approach the array of items which glittered like pirate's treasure before them.

Isabel, deeply moved seeing the children's evident joy, mouthed an inaudible *thank you* to Nathan who in return nodded with a wide smile. The children enthusiastically picked the objects up and observed them, turning them round and round in their hands, watching the light bounce off the shiny surfaces of the metal crockery and waving the fabrics in the air like huge flags in a parade. Mary and Sally, the two older girls in the group having just turned twelve, tried on the jewellery and wrapped their slender bodies in the colourful clothes. Theo picked up a coin and bit it to find out that he was able to bite through it. He pouted in disappointment.

'Look! A crown,' Tina said unable to contain the thrill which filled the room through her high-pitched scream. She got hold of it and lifted it high in the air for everyone to look at.

'It looks so real!' Rosy exclaimed and tried to touch it too, but Tina teased her by jumping up and down, her hand held high above her head. Rosy was too small to reach though she tiptoed and stretched her arms up towards the glinting crown but Tina took no heed and continued to keep the crown out of Rosy's grasp.

'This crown belongs to the king of Lion's Mane,' Nathan announced. 'Today I am announcing the roles each of you will be allocated for our play,' he said.

'Who is the king?' the boys asked in unison, their voices booming, and they looked at each other making poses of grandeur, their heads held high as if the crown was already atop of their heads.

Nathan took the crown and looked around the room. Isabel had no idea who Nathan had in mind for the role. They had thought of the play together, on one of their nights, sitting side by side in her bed, enclosed in his warm arms, kissing every now and then and laughing at the funny scenes they had devised. Nathan then put it on paper, rushing before they forgot the lines they had come up with, and then he had the responsibility to decide on the casting of each actor. Thus, she was totally unaware of the final outcome, so she was too on the edge of her seat along with all the children who looked at Nathan with wide round eyes, chewing on their lips or nails.

'The king is going to be Tommy,' Nathan announced and all the children quietened. Tommy seated in the corner of the room looked up in all amazement. He was the most reserved boy, hardly ever smiled. Isabel was not surprised; Nathan had told her time and again that he discerned a special spark in the boy's eyes when he was performing. The other children, however, looked on open-mouthed, clearly not quite believing their teacher's choice.

'Congratulations Tommy!' Isabel and Ms Cabbage both exclaimed clapping, smiling encouragingly at him. Tommy hesitated and blushed profusely as no one else seemed to share their mirth. The rest of the children looked at each other and a few of the older children started whispering. Tommy reluctantly got up and slowly walked towards Nathan. He stopped right in front him and gazed at him, pushing out his chest, straightening his shoulders and stretching his body as if he was trying to look taller.

'Tommy, you are selected to be the brave King of Lion's Mane,' Nathan announced in all seriousness. 'You should protect this crown as you protect your people. You should always be just and fearless,' Nathan said and slowly placed the crown on Tommy's head which was a perfect fit. Tommy, then, made the deepest bow.

'I vow to honour this crown. Thank you for the trust, Mr Dunkan,' he said in the loudest voice they had ever heard him speak. Isabel, Ms Cabbage and the rest of the children were stunned by the transformation and after a brief silence everybody started clapping and cheering for Tommy, their valiant king. They all surrounded him, some tapping him on his back with adulation and some hugging him to congratulate him. Isabel had never seen Tommy smiling so broadly from ear to ear and her heart fluttered with happiness. Nathan had worked his magic again spreading happiness to those who had the fortuitous luck to be close to him. She felt so lucky for crossing paths with such a generous and thoughtful man. Even if it was only for a little while longer, she knew well that he had changed her, healed her broken heart, helped her feel again after the numbness and emptiness she experienced with her husband's demise.

'Fire! Fire!' the scared scream of Ms Jeckins, the school's cook, interrupted the cheering and Isabel's deep thoughts. Isabel stepped outside the parlour to the sight of smoke, thick and strangling, surrounding them fast. Ms Jeckins ran to Isabel trembling, tears in her eyes.

'I don't know where the smoke is coming from!' she shouted frantically and ran for the door. Isabel scooped to the floor and touched it with the back of her hand; a great heat emanated through it.

'The fire is in the basement,' she shouted. 'We need to take the children out immediately.'

To her urgent appeal Nathan and Ms Cabbage took immediate action. With great control and focus they instructed the children to form a line and cover their noses with their sleeves as the smoke had now reached the parlour. The children started coughing and spluttering, their eyes suddenly streaming with tears, sore and red-rimmed, and as the thick smoke filled the room struggling to breathe. Isabel looked in the direction of the kitchen and saw flames licking the walls, destroying everything she had worked so hard for. A cold sweat covered her face and she started shaking but she knew well it was not the time to freeze.

'Now, let's all hurry out! Stay close to each other!' Isabel heard Nathan instructing and she could feel her legs moving again. Nathan, Isabel and Ms Cabbage led the children to the exit and when they had safely left the building, they all formed a huge embrace. The children were all badly shaken but to Isabel's relief nobody was injured. The orange of the blazes reflected on their teary eyes.

'Everything is gone,' Tina said with a sniffle and closed her eyes in despair. Isabel hugged her tight.

'We will fix everything all over again. I promise you,' Isabel said and smiled encouragingly at the children whose smoked faces and whimpers broke her heart.

'Isn't that Nathan Dunkan?' Isabel heard people commenting. She observed with quiet admiration how Nathan was calling upon passersby for help and in no time, he managed to assemble enough people to form a huge relay of supporters. Knowing that the "Jimmy Braiders" would not intervene in a timely manner, Nathan, with poise and control, instructed a few men to locate the hatch of the cistern on the road from which to collect water. They lifted it hurriedly and volunteers from the neighbouring houses and passersby fetched and passed buckets of water fighting the raging fire that was now visible through the windows. Isabel overcome with gratitude for Nathan's presence on this difficult day quickly realised all his efforts to salvage her school seemed futile. She pushed back the frustration of tears which threatened to burst from her. And in their place, a powerful warmth spread through her; Nathan was proving his genuine care for her and for the children and that was something she could no longer ignore.

'Tommy! Where is Tommy?' Isabel heard Ms Cabbage calling. Isabel's heart banged through her chest fast.

'Tommy!' she also screamed at the top of her lungs. Nathan ran to her when he realised the commotion.

'Has anyone seen Tommy?' Nathan asked.

'He was next to me but then he noticed his crown fell on our way out…' Theo said reluctantly.

Isabel and Nathan faced each other knowingly. Isabel

closed her eyes in despair tasting the acrid smoke in her throat and when she opened them Nathan was already gone. Her heart thumped uncontrollably and her whole body started trembling as she turned to see Nathan running towards the burning building. She made to move and scream at him to stop but her voice failed her. Images of her reckless husband and the feelings of despair and sadness came pouring into her soul and her legs could not hold her anymore. She fell to the ground as everything around her started spinning. She heard the wild gasps and the panicked screams of people as Nathan passed through the flaming door.

Nathan disappeared into the burning building. Isabel was going to lose him. *Not Nathan, God! Not him too,* she pleaded, and she could hardly see any more blinded by the tears that had flooded her eyes. *Why do you have to take from me all that I love?* she thought in despair.

She held her breath, until, after what seemed like an eternity, she saw Nathan stumbling out, his shirt torn and his face scorched by the heat, carrying Tommy in his arms.

People started cheering and clapping and Isabel was able to catch her breath again, though that she was neither relieved nor happy. She was enraged with Nathan. She suddenly hated him for the pain he had almost caused her. No! She didn't want to relive the despair of the past. Neither her body nor her mind would be able to endure another trauma. *Tommy,* she thought and a surge of energy boosted her body.

She, finally, found the strength to stand up and ran towards Nathan.

'Tommy!' she shouted without looking at Nathan. 'Let him lie on the ground,' she ordered, and she immediately started her efforts to revive the boy. 'Some water, please. And someone, please call a doctor,' she pleaded addressing the crowd. A man approached her with a bucket of water and Isabel cleaned the boy's head and she started massaging his body.

'Tommy! Please open your eyes,' she cried out and, the boy, as if he heard her, moved his head and began to mumble incoherent words. Isabel pulled him onto her lap and held him tight.

'You are safe now,' she said.

'Hurray!' all the children cheered. 'Mr Dunkan is a hero,' Tina shouted to the sound of which Isabel felt bile climbing her throat. She just tried to focus her attention on the children, choosing to ignore Nathan and the adverse feelings his presence was now causing her.

'Ms Cabbage!' she shouted. 'We will take the children to my house.'

'We need some coaches,' Ms Cabbage said.

'Leave that to me. I will find transport,' Nathan offered and he walked through the crowd that had quickly surrounded them.

Chapter 21

Nathan was perplexed. Ever since they got to Isabel's home, she was ignoring him. She treated him as if he was invisible. He could understand she was devastated because of the loss of her school and now the chaos at her house. The staff frantically moved up and down the stairs carrying linen and food. The children were running around exploring the rooms and playing, seeming almost carefree after the disaster. Ms Cabbage in vain was struggling to control the havoc, running behind the children, scolding them when they picked up and curiously examined hand-painted vases and delicate ornamental statues of labradors and poodles. Isabel was, also, too busy giving instructions, walking in and out of rooms, changing the layout of the furniture, making a great effort to create enough space to accommodate the children's sleeping needs. Nathan was also trying as much as he could to help the situation, but he felt like a pariah, almost unwanted. He needed to speak to Isabel, but he couldn't find her alone. He patiently waited for a chance because something was amiss, and he needed to understand. What he did earlier that day had frightened the life out of him, but he had saved Tommy. The dangerous situation had presented little choice really. Nathan felt responsible for Tommy's innocent recklessness since he had made him swear that he would take good care of his crown.

'Nathan,' Tommy's voice interrupted his thoughts. Nathan kneeled to be on his level. Tommy fell into his arms and embraced him tightly.

'I am sorry Nathan. I am so sorry I put your life in danger,' he said in tears.

Nathan caressed the boy's hair tenderly and then offered his hankie to him.

'This is too smelly,' Tommy commented wrinkling his cute little nose and Nathan chuckled.

'This is how we all smell right now. We were almost all baked,' Nathan said, and Tommy giggled.

'That is why Ms Pearlbrooke insists we all have a bath,' Tommy admitted.

'Tommy, I need you to promise me something. Don't you ever risk your life again. I am not scolding you. I am simply saying that we love you, and it will break our hearts if anything ever happens to you,' Nathan said, and he observed how Tommy's eyes grew huge, and his cheeks blushed.

'My parents never once said that they loved me. They never cared for me. I am a burden, a useless worm, as they call me. When Ms Pearlbrooke told them that I could stay in her school, they didn't blink twice before they got rid of me. But I do not despair. Ms Pearlbrooke became my mother and now I have a father too. You,' he said and gave Nathan a little peck on the cheek.

'I will always be here for you Tommy,' Nathan said deeply moved. At that moment, he could not but feel grateful for all the love his parents had given him and his sister even for the short time they had together. The sweet memories of his mother putting him to bed and reading him stories and the endless walks with his father in the woods eased his pain of their loss. Nathan wanted to give this comfort to Tommy. In fact, he had come to love and care for all the children in the school. He was as ready to commit to them as Isabel was in devoting her life to them. His body suddenly tensed. Isabel's strange behaviour, had him worried. While everybody glorified him as a hero for saving Tommy, Isabel chose silence. She had never been that distant before. She was probably blaming him for Tommy lagging behind. *Yes! That is quite possible,* he thought and now more than ever he was determined to confront her. She couldn't be mad with him forever. Surely, she could understand that his intentions were only to boost Tommy's confidence, to lift the spirits of that sad little boy who hardly ever smiled by gifting him the crown.

He determinately marched through the house to find her.

'Where is Ms Pearlbrooke?' he asked a maid who passed him hurryingly carrying a pile of smoke-damaged and dirty clothes.

'I believe she is in her study, sir,' she answered.

Nathan finally had the chance he was looking for. He hurried to her and with a quick knock on the door he burst into the room. Isabel was alone and Nathan locked the door behind him making sure that they were not going to be interrupted. Isabel was not taken aback by Nathan's somewhat bold invasion of her privacy. Her gaze was steady and cold which made Nathan freeze.

'I think you owe me an explanation,' he managed to

say, trying to maintain his equanimity.

'I owe you nothing, Mr Dunkan,' Isabel answered. 'I thank you for your help today, but we can manage without you from now on. Have a good night, sir,' she said and turned her back on him, looking outside her window.

Nathan was now boiling with anger. Isabel was not only being unreasonable; she was also being quite offensive. In any other circumstance he would have left the room, and vanished forever, but he loved the damn woman. He was not abandoning her, nor the children and he was going to make her see.

'You are being unreasonable!' he scolded her. 'I understand you may be blaming me for Tommy's foolishness to try and retrieve his crown, but…'

Nathan didn't manage to finish. Isabel surged towards him and with her fists she started hitting his chest.

'Damn you! You foolish man! How dare you? How dare you risk your life like this,' she screamed trembling like a leaf. Nathan startled by her violent outburst took hold of her two wrists and tried to steady her but Isabel was enraged. She continued to push him away trying to escape his grip. She was like a wild beast, in a trance, not cognisant of the reality Nathan felt.

'You never once thought of me! Did you? The pain you were inflicting on me through your heroic actions, the constant fear pounding at me. How could you David? How could you? Damn you. I hate you!' she shouted again at the top of her lungs.

Nathan finally understood. He fought to put her in his arms and when he did, embraced her tightly, whispering in her ear.

'I am not David. I am here. You have not lost me.' He

repeated the words until finally Isabel stopped fighting him. She started relaxing in his arms though her whimpers broke his heart.

'I am sorry,' he said to her. 'I am deeply sorry, I scared you, that I made you feel unsafe.' He kissed her forehead. 'I am here and I am alive.'

'David died in a burning building. Though, everybody reassured him that nobody was inside, he still decided to jump into the flames. He was always putting himself in dangerous situations, taking risks, gloating about his fearless nature while I was petrified every single day of losing him, hurting deeply by his inconsiderate, thoughtless actions. He simply didn't care for me. You know what's worse? They never found him in the debris. There was nothing left of him. It's as if he vanished into thin air. Sometimes I doubt he ever existed. I second guess my own sanity. Maybe it was all a nightmare but there is no comfort in that either,' Isabel confessed.

'I am so deeply sorry, Isabel. I am sorry I made you relive the pain. I am here, alive, hugging you and I promise you I will not risk my life thoughtlessly ever again simply because I care for you and for the children too much.'

Isabel put her arms around his waist and held him tight. 'I know you do. I know you felt responsible for Tommy. I am so grateful you saved his life but the thought of losing you… was unbearable. Please take good care of yourself, Nathan Dunkan,' she said and faced him with a thin smile.

Nathan didn't want to leave Isabel's house that evening. He wanted to stay with her and support her, make her feel safe. The only thing that gave him comfort was that now he knew without a doubt. Isabel Pearlbrooke loved him too.

Chapter 22

The situation was bleak. The devastation of the school was total and the repairs by the latest estimations would take a fortune and maybe months to complete. Nathan was getting desperate to spend time with Isabel alone, to hug her, kiss her and enjoy a night together but it was simply impossible. He visited Isabel every day, helping her with any errand which she required and any job, however menial just so he could be close to her. But the demands were endless.

Isabel required a lot of money and fast but even finding the funds for her would not solve his problem. He simply missed her, craved for her. His brain was working hard trying to find solutions as he entered her house that morning, thus, Isabel jumping out on him in all her enthusiasm was the last thing he expected as he walked into her study. He lost his balance as she collided with him and they both ended up falling flat on the floor. Isabel cackled unable to hold back her delight and Nathan joined in, her laughter infectious after so much desolation and angst.

'Are you alright?' Nathan asked still lying on his back, trying to get a hold of his breath… and his composure.

'I am more than alright,' Isabel answered in mirth rolling onto him and laying her body flat along the length of his torso. This had been exactly what Nathan longed for, only he preferred them to be naked in a warm soft bed. Isabel kissed him passionately.

'I miss you so much,' she whispered in his ear as she broke their kiss and rolled off him to stand up. She, then, extended her hand to help Nathan up too.

'You seem happy today,' Nathan commented.

'I am very happy, indeed,' Isabel chirped gleefully. She went to her desk and picked up a piece of paper. She handed it to Nathan to read. Nathan knew exactly what he was looking at. He had signed the document himself that very morning, but he would never reveal it to Isabel nor to anyone else. He pretended to read through the document, scanning the words quickly and acted surprised, and quite convincingly so. He was a great actor after all.

'I received this early this morning. The amount donated affords me the greatest relief. I have already sent a missive to my contractor to speed up the building and refurbishing process, hire more workers. I do not know who the Baron of Witney is but I am truly obliged to him.'

'Ms Pearlbrooke, I do believe you have an admirer who is most definitely enamoured with you. Should I be worried?'

'Worried? I can't recall ever meeting the man. I will ask Lydia and Catherine if they are acquainted. Maybe they know his family, know of him. In fact, I am going to send them a note immediately,' she said and sat behind her desk. She took a clean piece of paper and dipped her quill into the inkwell.

'Now what shall I write? Should I mention the sum?'

She wondered. 'I shouldn't mention the amount. I am not even sure whether the kind gentleman would want people to know of his grand and generous gesture. What do you think?' she asked, facing Nathan who smiled looking at her, admiring her beauty though he didn't miss how tired she looked.

'Isabel, where did you sleep last night?' he asked.

'Where I have slept every night for the past seven days,' she commented while writing her short note.

'And where would that be?' Nathan insisted.

'Here, in my study. It is warm and quiet,' Isabel answered, seemingly unbothered.

Nathan looked around the room. He could only see two upholstered armchairs. There was not even a settee in the room. Nathan couldn't keep at bay a nasty feeling. He noticed a blanket neatly folded on one of the armchairs.

'Please do not tell me you sleep in this armchair,' Nathan asked with urgency.

'I do,' Isabel answered with her attention to the task at hand.

Nathan cursed himself for the oversight. How did he miss this all these days?

'And may I ask why?' he continued calmly, though deep inside he was boiling with rage.

'I have ceded my bed to Ms Cabbage who shares it with Tina. I begged her to stay with us to help me with the children and she gladly agreed. It was the least I could do for the poor woman who is now deprived of her own household. She is taking care of the children, attending to their needs at every hour of the day, or during the night as some of the younger ones are calling out to her with nightmares. Thus, she is giving me all the time I need to deal with the financial issues, fundraising and all the other technicalities which come with the rebuild. Her presence here is invaluable. She has been a God send, and I am most grateful to her.'

Nathan shook his head with resentment. This was preposterous.

'And for how long are you planning to keep this arrangement?' he asked her.

'Indefinitely,' Isabel answered, raising her shoulders and then added, 'Until we are safely able to move the children back to the school.'

'This is not realistic. I hope you do understand that sleeping in an armchair is not a sustainable solution,' Nathan said exasperated.

'Hmm, perhaps I should order a settee. Though, spending money on unnecessary items is not wise. However, with the baron's kind donation we can afford it. You are right!' Isabel exclaimed enthusiastically. 'I should write to Mr Woodbird to order a settee. I should, also, order new beds and....' Isabel continued mumbling inaudibly while writing down her order.

'Why don't you come and stay with me?' Nathan blurted without thinking it through.

Isabel stopped writing and looked at him with an arched eyebrow. 'Are you jesting?' she asked.

Nathan shallowed hard. He had never invited anyone to his house. Only Alistair knew the truth about him and the whereabouts of his residence and even he never paid Nathan a visit. But Isabel, he surmised, was in great need. He could not let her live like this.

'I am quite serious, Isabel. You cannot continue like this. You will exhaust yourself. Let me take care of you.

Come to my home. You will enjoy a nice long quiet bath and you can lay your weary body on my soft mattress,' Nathan said. As he continued to speak, his excitement grew with the prospect. His idea appealed to him more and more, however, Isabel didn't seem convinced yet. 'We will finally get to spend some time together, alone,' he added.

The quietness was interrupted by the stomps of running children outside Isabel's study. Soon after, the thunderous clatter of a tumbled piece of furniture and the breaking of glass alerted them both to jump up and move towards the study's door. They rushed into the corridor to find Theo flat on the ground with a vase smashed into tiny pieces next to him and the flowers it had contained sprawled limp and broken across his tummy and atop of his head. Nigel was hiding behind a curtain, giggling, unable to contain himself. Isabel checked on Theo while two maids tried to pick up the pieces and clean up the mess. Amid the commotion, Isabel faced Nathan and shouted, 'If your offer still stands, I will. Tonight!' which gave Nathan the greatest pleasure.

Chapter 23

Isabel nervously twisted the clasp of her little leather handbag over and over while waiting for Nathan to collect her that evening after his performance at the theatre. They had agreed to make their way to his home together. How did she agree to this insanity? She had no idea where Nathan lived. In her desperation to escape the unbearably difficult situation of her own home, it didn't occur to her to ask where he resided. What if the area he lived in was of ill-repute or dangerous. Was she dressed humbly enough not to attract attention? Moreover, she was putting her reputation on the line, going to a man's house alone. *He comes to yours. How is that any different?* her own mind argued. She surmised that decency was not the essence of what bothered her. What did plague her? Isabel had noticed Nathan's reluctance even though it was he who suggested that she stayed at his house. He said the words, but they initially sounded unsure, guarded. Maybe he too felt that this decision was too intimate given the nature of their relationship, their arrangement. Residing at his home, for however short or long a time, would certainly be breaking the rules of their contract or were his concerns more to do with his residence? Perhaps his home was a modest one which embarrassed him. Most likely he regretted asking her, but she was so desperate to be alone with him that she didn't give him much choice to withdraw his offer. But by now, Nathan, she was sure, must have known she was the kind of woman who could live by simple means. He knew she had voyaged on board ships for months. And she had even described to him how she had slept under the starry sky on a pile of leaves that David had been gathering for them on their way to Bombay from Egypt. Though it had not been the most comfortable sleep, she had endured it with grace and patience. *Certainly, Nathan's bed must be softer and cosier than some leafage,* she thought with an anticipation close to uncontrollable delight.

Even if he had a glimmer of regret, she was determined to show him her appreciation for everything he had done for her all this time. Nathan Dunkan was her guardian angel. And she pondered, she was foolishly going to let her angel fly away when their contract expired but what choice did she have? She was getting weak in her resolve. She suspected that she loved him, but she was not willing to contemplate the idea. She had been hurt in the past and she was unwilling to endure any more pain. Nathan told her numerous times how he prioritised his writing over heart matters. He was ambitious and he dreamed of his plays becoming known worldwide. And he deserved it. He was so talented, and Isabel was certain Nathan would find the success he worked so hard to achieve. She thought of how she would admire him from afar and maybe in her older days she would confess to her closest friends how she was once in love with the most famous playwright of their time.

The knock on the door interrupted her thoughts. She

opened the door slowly and tiptoed outside.

'We should be very quiet,' Isabel whispered as she closed the front door behind her making sure there wasn't a single noise.

'Are you escaping from your own house?' Nathan asked with a chuckle.

She was escaping!

'In fact, I am. I only told Ms Cabbage I was spending the night away and she was relieved with the news. She was afraid that my back was going to be deformed by sleeping upright. She said that I was going to turn into an adorable hunchback.'

Nathan guffawed and Isabel shushed him.

'Goodness me. The whole neighbourhood will now know about my departure. So where is the carriage?' Isabel asked scanning the street.

'We will not be needing one,' Nathan answered. 'I don't live far from your street,' he explained, avoiding Isabel's raised eyebrows. 'Is this the only bag you are carrying?'

'I am only staying for the one night,' Isabel answered still trying to process the proximity of his house to her own. *How is that even possible?* she wondered. *Surely actors do not earn that much, do they?*

'A single night's sleep will not prevent that hunch from growing on your back,' Nathan said and he caressed Isabel's cheek. 'Now, let us go. Mr Thorns is looking forward to meeting you and he has prepared a wonderful meal for our arrival.'

'Mr Thorns lives with you?' Isabel asked even more perplexed. 'I thought you lived alone.'

'No, Mr Thorns moved with me to London when I left my village. I was very young back then. He wanted to make sure I was taking care of myself. He is a wonderful man. I am sure you are going to find him most agreeable,' Nathan said and stopped in front of a three-storey house with a pastel-coloured stucco façade. 'We are here.'

Isabel's mouth dropped. Nathan's house was literally two streets away from hers. In fact, she walked past the row of residences quite often. She was always admiring the elegant wrought iron balconies with the unique petal-like patterns. She wanted to ask him so many questions, but she wasn't sure where to start.

'Come, let's go inside,' Nathan said, and Isabel once again discerned a hint of reluctance in his voice. As they climbed the wide stone steps the front door opened wide and an older gentleman in a butler's uniform welcomed them with a wide smile.

'Welcome, welcome. Hurry inside. It is too cold today.'

'Isabel, allow me to introduce Mr Thorns,' Nathan said.

'I am very pleased to make your acquaintance Mr Thorns. I have heard so many wonderful things about you. I feel I already know you,' Isabel said, taking an instant liking to the man whose eyes revealed his kind nature. She, then, started exploring the space. The house was grand indeed, but it was practically empty. The entrance hall was colourless with no distinct oil colours and there were no pieces of furniture. As they walked along the long stark corridor, she noticed the complete absence of art on the walls.

'We are dining in my study,' Nathan said and as he opened the door Isabel's impression of the place changed. The room was beautifully decorated. The green wallpaper was of the finest quality and the emerald silk curtains framed elegantly the windows, tall and imposing, the evening dusk glowing through the panes. The mahogany desk was an impressive piece of furniture along with the built-in bookcase which covered the whole back wall from the wooden floor to the beautifully carved ceiling that mirrored the intricate design of the room's carpet. Isabel felt excited looking at the wide selection of leatherbound book collections. Some of them were lying on the floor, scattered open at intervals. *Nathan is a true booklover,* she thought, just as she was. She had a lot to explore and to discover about the house and this man.

'Our dinner will be served here,' Nathan said, pointing at a beautiful round ebony table complete with carved chairs intricate with painted decorations. 'My dining room is not yet furnished,' Nathan said and cleared his throat awkwardly. Isabel just then thought of Lydia's comment about Nathan. He indeed had ties to the nobility, that was obvious. But the lack of staff and furniture could only mean one thing. His family had financial troubles. That made perfect sense. Nathan pulled out a chair for Isabel to sit down. She had so many questions but she was resolved to be discreet and avoid bringing the unpleasant matter to surface.

'This is a very beautiful room,' Isabel commented, 'And your book collection looks quite impressive.'

'Thank you,' Nathan said. 'This room and my bedroom were decorated by my mother. Unfortunately, she died before she finished the refurbishment of the house. I am very private, and I hardly ever have guests visiting me, thus, I never felt the need to finish what she started,' Nathan said and brushed his chin with scepticism.

'And Mr Thorns takes care of the entire house all by himself?' Isabel asked.

'No. We have Mrs Smith who comes every day and cleans. She doesn't stay with us though. Mr Thorns does most of the cooking. He loves it. And I am lucky because he is an exceptional cook. Ah, and here he is!' Nathan exclaimed and immediately stood up to help the elderly man with the big tray he was carrying. They both worked fast setting the table and serving the food. A big oval platter of venison and vegetables, a plate of cheese, and a basket of freshly baked bread made Isabel's mouth water.

'Mmm, the food smells delicious! Would you like to join us, Mr Thorns?' Isabel asked politely.

'I thank you my lady but I would rather take my leave now. The day has been long and I am not a young man anymore,' Mr Thorns said with a sweet smile, and he left the room quickly with an admirable agility for his age.

Isabel dived into her meal with appetite. Every bite pleased her palate immensely.

'Mmm, this is divine,' she commented. 'I was famished.'

'Haven't you had anything to eat all day?' Nathan asked worryingly.

'I don't think I did. I had such a busy day today,' Isabel admitted, and she didn't miss Nathan's furrowed eyebrows. 'Don't worry about me, Nathan. I am doing well,' she said and smiled at him encouragingly.

'No, you're not! You don't eat and you don't sleep properly,' he scolded her. 'That is it! You are staying here for as long as you need. I will make sure you take care of yourself, ' he said strictly and Isabel's heart, much to her surprise filled with warmth and joy. Nathan cared for her deeply. *Could he love me too*? she thought but she immediately forced herself to dismiss the idea.

'We will see,' she said, and her eyes fell for the first time on a painting of a beautiful couple over the fireplace. The man looked a lot like Nathan, but Nathan had the woman's green eyes. The woman wore a simple yet beautiful light dress of green silk that brought out the colour of her eyes and the man was dressed in a slick riding habit. The background indicated that they were in the countryside, as tall poplar trees and wildflowers surrounded them.

'These are my parents,' Nathan said.

'You have your mother's eyes,' Isabel commented and she looked at Nathan intently. 'You are so handsome,' she blurted, and her cheeks burned red. 'Have you got any siblings?' she asked, clearing her throat, trying to change the subject and hide her embarrassment.

'I have an older sister. Her name is Carolina. She lives back home in the village with her husband and my two nephews. They also take care of the estate,' Nathan revealed, taking Isabel by surprise. *Estate?* Isabel was dying to ask but she held back once again.

'I don't visit them as often as I would like due to my theatrical obligations but one day I would love to return,' Nathan admitted, and Isabel noticed the glow in his eyes.

'Would you leave London? How about your acting career?'

'I like acting, but my ultimate goal is to simply write and have my plays acted all over the world. It's a somewhat wild and ambitious aspiration, I know,' he said.

'Not at all. You are very talented. I know you are going to be very successful, Nathan. I have complete faith in you,' Isabel uttered.

'Thank you, Ms Pearlbrooke. But I suspect you are a little biased,' Nathan jested.

'I am your biggest admirer, Mr Dunkan and rightly so,'

Isabel intoned. Their intense staring in the moment made Isabel's heart pound uncontrollably. Any second and she was going to confess things she was certain to regret immediately such as how she was in love with him. There was no point hiding the truth from her own self. But as long as Nathan didn't know she was safe. *If I don't admit the feeling, it doesn't exist,* she said to herself unsure of the veracity of her belief.

'Whether I succeed or not I wouldn't want my children to grow in London. I cherish my carefree childhood in the countryside, within a small community where I felt safe and loved especially after my parents' demise.'

The mention of having children and raising them in the countryside shook Isabel to the core. His words hurt her, but she managed to veil her disappointment and pain. She continued smiling at him and listened to his childhood stories but deep inside she was melting. Of course, Nathan dreamt of having a family. What did she expect really? The man never promised her anything. *I am such a foolish woman,* she said to herself and decided to bury all her feelings deep inside. No one would ever know how she really felt. No one!

'Isabel? Are you alright? I lost you for a while,' Nathan said, and Isabel shook her head as if she was throwing all her negative thoughts away.

'How did your parents die?' Isabel asked.

'It was a road accident,' Nathan said, and his eyes immediately darkened to the memory. 'They were returning from London, and something scared their horses. They became feral, trying to break loose from the carriage. The driver was incapable of calming them despite his greatest efforts and he was the first to hit the ground which miraculously actually saved him. My father, my mother and one servant didn't have time to escape the carriage. The horses ran wild and in a close turn, the carriage capsized, and it was dragged over a cliff. The driver, though badly injured, walked to the village and notified the residents. The men of our community formed a rescue team. With long ropes they worked tirelessly and selflessly until they managed to reach the bottom of the cliff, but no one had survived the fall. I was never allowed to see the bodies of my parents. My sister begged to see them and because she was seventeen at the time the family indulged her but for months after I could hear her screams at night, nightmares haunted her,' Nathan said and paused, he leaned forward onto the table and hid his face behind his palms. Isabel immediately stood up and went to him. She hugged him tightly.

'I am so sorry, Nathan. I didn't mean to cause you pain,' she said and kissed him tenderly over his hair. Nathan then pulled her onto his lap and gave her a kiss.

'It is alright. I need to confess my pain to you. I feel relieved talking to the person I trust the most in my life. I am so lucky I have met you, Isabel,' he said and kissed her again, more passionately this time, with hunger and a deep longing. Isabel melted in his embrace and wished for the moment to never end. She was in a beautiful room, with her very handsome and interesting lover, enjoying the best meal of her life. She had so much to celebrate for and she was determined to enjoy the time they had together.

'Do you know that you are the very first person to visit my house here in London?' Nathan confessed while nudging her nose.

'Am I? No other woman has ever slept in your bed?' Isabel asked, kissing his eyebrows.

'You are the very first and I can't wait to take you there.'

Nathan opened the door of his bedroom and gestured Isabel to walk inside. The room was the most beautiful indeed. The walls were covered with beige wallpaper with golden leaves, unparallel to anything Isabel had seen before. The dark-blue curtains were heavy brocade, and the bed was a true work of art, with carved daises and roses on the posters. Isabel could not help but let her fingers gently run over the intricate design. She scanned the room, and she found her leather bag already neatly placed on a table and its content, her only dress, was hanged on a valet stand ready to be worn the next day.

'I should thank Mr Thorns for taking care of my dress,' Isabel commented.

'Is this the only item of clothing you brought with you?' Nathan asked. 'Didn't you bring a nightgown?'

'Do I need one?' Isabel asked suggestively and she started unbuttoning her dress and then she unlaced her stays slowly releasing her breasts for Nathan to look at. Nathan did not move, nor did he breathe. He looked at Isabel with his eyes half open. Isabel removed all her clothing and stood naked in front of him.

'Nathan, please remove your clothes and lie on the bed,' she requested, and Nathan gladly and hurryingly complied. He undressed in seconds and dived, onto his back first, into his bed. Isabel walked slowly and observed how her magnificent man was ready for her, already hard.

'I love your readiness, Mr Dunkan,' she said as she sat next to him letting her hand caress his manhood softly.

Nathan smiled at her comment. Isabel, then, leaned in and with her lips and tongue she ran up and down the length of his shaft. Nathan writhed to the sensation and moaned with pleasure. She, then, straddled him and lowered herself slowly onto his erection. She started moving up and down his length, rhythmically, enjoying the sensation as her pleasure grew. But then, a thought crossed her mind that made her stop. She opened her eyes and looked at Nathan with awe. Nathan stilled, looked back quite perplexed.

'Why did you stop?' he asked out of breath.

'It is you, isn't it? You made the donation. You are the Baron of Witney!' she exclaimed enthusiastically.

'Isabel, this is not the right time to discuss this. Not while I am inside you. Please woman, move,' he pleaded but Isabel was determined to get the truth out of him even if she had to torture him a little bit.

She slowly raised and lowered herself deeply to his stiffness.

'Yes, that's it,' Nathan cried out but Isabel stopped again.

'If this is what you want Nathan, you have to tell me the truth,' she said and refused to move her hips, leaving him wanting more.

'You are a stubborn woman,' Nathan said and with a sudden, strong move he managed to get hold of Isabel, roll her over and pull her body beneath his. Isabel, though defeated, she chuckled.

'Do you want to know the truth, Isabel? Yes, I am the Baron of Witney,' he said and tried to kiss her, but Isabel held his face in her palms.

'But the amount Nathan. It's too much,' she said quite moved by the revelation.

'Don't you see, Isabel? There is nothing I wouldn't do for you. I'm…'

But Isabel didn't let him finish. She pulled his face to hers and kissed him hungrily. Their bodies merged as one and they lost themselves in their passionate lovemaking.

Chapter 24

Nathan was determined. He was going to propose to Isabel, and he wasn't taking no for an answer. The past month, during which they practically lived together, was the happiest of his life. He was acutely aware of his feelings for Isabel but finding her in the kitchen a week ago, helping Mr Thorns with the cooking and seeing them talking and laughing together, encouraged him most positively to make this life-changing decision. He knew it was not going to be an easy task to persuade her. She had been hurt immensely in the past and, rightly so, she was protecting her heart. But he was going to fight for her. *There is no escape Ms Pearlbrooke*, he thought as he looked at his mother's ring once again making sure that it had been properly polished at Rundell and Bridge, the most prestigious jewellery shop. He wanted only the best for his future wife.

Tonight was the night. Mr Thorns already knew of his intentions, and he momentarily teared to the news. He promised to prepare the best meal for them and got to the task immediately.

'What have you got there?' Alistair asked as he entered their dressing room at the theatre.

'I have got some news, my friend. Tonight, I am proposing to Isabel,' Nathan announced with a wide smile, his extended hand displaying the engagement ring for Alistair to see. Alistair's reaction was not the one anticipated. He pressed his lips in a thin line and shook his head with resentment.

'Oh no, no! I am afraid my friend this is not possible. This is the absolute worst time to make such a decision,' Alistair spluttered.

'What the hell do you mean?' Nathan protested.

'I have some great news too. I was just talking to Mr Donahue. Your play, Nathan, is to travel the world as you have always dreamt. We are touring Europe and then sailing to New York. You did it my friend! You are a success,' Alistair cheered but Nathan found it impossible to share his mirth.

'When are we expected to leave?' he asked, his gut squeezing in both excitement and dread.

'The 27th of July is departure day.'

Nathan closed his eyes unable to process the irony. That was the date their contract ended. He chuckled, shaking his head.

'The tour will take months,' Nathan said and he started pacing back and forth, the length of the dressing room, quite upset.

'A year,' Alistair offered. 'Nathan, this is your dream. Why aren't you celebrating?'

'I can't leave Isabel and the children for so long. I can't be away from them. They need me.'

'Isabel and the children? What children, Nathan? You don't have any children. The students in Isabel's school are not your responsibility. They have parents already. Do you hear yourself? As for Isabel, if she loves you, she will wait for you.'

Alistair's calm supposition, of course, made perfect sense, but Nathan could not imagine himself spending a single day apart from Isabel, let alone an entire year. He needed her.

'No, it's impossible. You should go without me,' Nathan said.

'You know well that Donahue will never agree to this. He wants you in the lead role and especially now he is going to invest so heavily in you. Do you think he will agree to someone else taking your place? Impossible and you know it well,' Alistair said in a desperate voice. 'Do not throw away everything you have worked so hard for, Nathan. Not for a woman,' he pleaded

'This is not any woman. I love her,' Nathan confessed, and the words gave him comfort and strength. This is what he needed in his life. Love and partnership. Not the wild chase of success.

'You are mad!' Alistair shouted. 'I can't speak to you anymore.'

Today's performance had not been the most successful, Nathan admitted on his way home. Alistair had been furious and hardly looked at him during the play. He could not convince anyone that he loved his friend on stage. The only scene that salvaged the situation was Alistair's menace over the duel. He hit him hard with any chance he got and gave him a black eye. Mary had to step in to stop them. Otherwise, he was certain to lose a tooth too. On the positive side, that scene gave them a standing ovation. Nathan regretted he had made his friend mad, but he was certain about his decision. He was staying with Isabel. Mr Donahue would have to take the play abroad without him.

Back at the house, the warmth of his home and the laughter and chatter of Isabel and Mr Thorns confirmed his decision.

'Nathan!' Isabel cried out seeing his black eye. She ran to him and Nathan pulled her into his arms.

'Nothing to worry about. Alistair got carried away on stage and he punched me a little harder than he ought to have, but we did get a standing ovation.'

Isabel kissed his eye softly. 'There. Are you feeling any better?' she asked.

'I am, thank you,' he said and squeezed her even tighter.

'You are going to crush me,' she giggled. 'Come in,' Isabel said. 'We have prepared everything for our dinner. Mr Thorns has exceeded himself today. He is in an incredible mood,' Isabel said cheerfully as she was served a vegetable velouté soup which smelt almost intoxicating. They both ate with great appetite while Isabel gave Nathan all the details of her day with the children and an update on the works in progress.

'Thus, everything is going very well. The children will return to school in a couple of weeks and finally you will rid of me,' Isabel said and grinned.

'Yes, about that Isabel. We need to discuss something.' Nathan started clearing his throat nervously. 'Leaving is no longer an option,' he said matter-of-factly.

'Am I to be held here as a hostage?' she jested.

Nathan peered at her intently. He took a deep breath and confessed.

'Isabel Pearlbrooke, I am madly in love with you! I can't let you go. I simply wish to spend the rest of my life with you,' he vehemently said, procuring the ring he held in his pocket.

Isabel looked at him in shock. She was speechless and her eyes filled with tears.

'Nathan, I can't,' she whispered with a little choke.

'Don't you love me?' Nathan asked without a single doubt in his mind about Isabel's feelings.

'You know I do,' she admitted without hesitation. 'I am deeply in love with you and that is exactly the reason I am not going to accept your offer.'

'Is it because you are afraid, I am going to hurt you? I will always try my best to keep you happy, Isabel. I am never, never, going to abandon or betray you. Please, trust me,' Nathan pleaded.

'I believe you, Nathan. I trust you with all my heart. That is not the reason I am not marrying you,' Isabel said with her tears now streaming down her cheeks.

'What plausible reason can you give me then?' Nathan asked.

'I am incapable of giving you children... you said that your dream is to move with your wife and children to the countryside. Thus, I can't be that wife. I wish I could...' she confessed and burst into incontrollable tears.

Nathan immediately stood up from his seat, rushed to her and fell on his knees to her side.

'Listen to me, Isabel. As I said to you before, having children doesn't necessarily mean that you must birth them. We both know well that there are so many orphaned children, love-deprived, suffering from loneliness. Tina is orphaned and Tommy's parents simply do not care for him. We can fill our house with children if you wish. We both have an abundance of love in our hearts to offer. I know you do. I have witnessed it. And being so close to you, and the children in your care, I have discovered how I too am capable of offering unconditional love and care. Please Isabel allow me to be part of this noble, blessed life with you.'

Isabel cupped his face gently in her hands and covered it with little pecks.

'I should set you free, but I can't. I love you so much,' Isabel admitted. 'Yes! My answer is yes. I will marry you, my love,' she said, and they hugged and kissed again and again until their lips felt numb. Then, Nathan slipped the ring onto Isabel's finger. It was a perfect fit.

'This is so beautiful.'

'It belonged to my mother. My sister found it in her jewellery box with a note addressed to me.' He reached into his pocket and took out a yellowed note paper which betrayed its aging.

> *To my son*
> *Do not look for love with your eyes*
> *But solely with your heart.*
> *A gift for your bride*
> *I love you, always*

Chapter 25

So much happiness was unfathomable for Isabel. She never imagined she could fall for a man again. Nathan not only loved her enough to accept her inability to give him children, but he was also completely immersed to her cause with the utmost care and dedication. They stayed up late talking, making plans for their joined future. They agreed that they would move to Witney and with them they would take Tommy and Tina; raise them both as their own for a start. Ms Cabbage would be promoted to head of the school and Isabel was going to hire one more teacher to help Ms Cabbage. Nathan was to quit acting, determined to focus on his true passion: writing. He felt that his latest success gave him that luxury. They would spend most months in the countryside, but Isabel would periodically come to London to oversee her school and ultimately open a second with the support of her new husband.

At the first glimpse of dawn Isabel decided there was no point staying in bed. Her excitement was too intense, and she had much to do. She had to write to Thalia and her parents. And then, she had to pay a visit to her friends at the duke's residence to tell them her news and ask for their help in preparing for the wedding. Catherine would most likely cry; Diana would jump up and down to the thrill of her announcement and Lydia would probably boast for bringing them back together.

Her wedding plans. Isabel thought and chuckled remembering how determined she was not to commit herself to any man ever again. But Nathan Dunkan was not any ordinary man. She turned to her side to face him and with a feather touch she caressed his strong torso making sure she didn't wake him. *At least one of us should be well rested,* she thought and withdrew her hand.

She got up, dressed in a hurry and sauntered along the empty corridors with a candle in hand, contemplating all the changes she could make to this beautiful residence as Nathan's wife. She wanted to finish the decorating and to furnish the rooms. She then remembered the two rooms on the top floor which already had beautiful cornices and architraves. Nathan's mother clearly intended those two bedrooms for her children and Isabel, of course, was still going to do just that and her heart fluttered with happiness. A bedroom in light blue colours for Tommy and a bedroom with lilac wallpaper and light green upholstery for Tina.

Isabel could not believe her ears when Nathan suggested raising Tommy and Tina as their own. In fact, she was already hoping for the possibility to do the very same thing. She had previously discussed her aspiration with Catherine who thought it was risky raising two young children with no husband to support them as a family, however, Lydia assured her that Isabel would be perfect for the role. They both promised to help her, and Diana offered to take them to the park and keep them company when life became too hectic for Isabel. With the new turn of events, though, Isabel was more determined than ever to make her dream a reality. She only hoped the children would be happy to live with them permanently.

Tommy and Tina were already close like brother and sister. Isabel described to Nathan that night how she had come upon them. Tommy's mother was a weak woman whose habitual drunkenness didn't allow her to care for her children and his father would disappear for months and hardly ever interacted with Tommy during the rare occasions that he was present in the family's life. Ms Cabbage had told Isabel about Tommy. She had met him in Bethnal Green in a small chapel where she used to teach children how to read and write on Wednesdays. Though not many children attended, Tommy was the only one who consistently showed up, trying hard to remember his letters. Ms Cabbage was really impressed with his tenacity and eagerness to learn. She had urged Isabel to come and meet the boy. Isabel had felt an instant connection with him and explained to him about her school and how he could live, learn and thrive there.

'They will never agree to it,' Tommy had answered disheartened, but Isabel was not to be so easily discouraged. She decided to meet with his family. She was extremely nervous as she entered the area where they lived; violent and shady. She disguised herself like she used to do when she was wandering the streets in Bombay with her friend, Agnes, helping the poor, only this time she had three male servants accompanying her. She asked her servants to wait outside the house to which they all expressed their strong objections, but Isabel knew well she had to face Tommy's parents alone. A woman alone would not pose any threat and they were more likely to listen to what she had to say.

Isabel remembered his father as a cruel, harsh man who called Tommy a bastard denying any ties with him despite his wife's slurred protests that didn't make much sense. Tommy hardly raised his head to look at Isabel while she was trying to explain who she was and what she did. It shocked her to remember how his father practically ushered them both outside the house, closing the door behind them with a violent bang that scared both Isabel and Tommy. Tommy had followed Isabel silently, refusing to answer any of her questions, always facing down at his feet. It took him days to start talking to Isabel at first and with persistence, patience and lots of love, Tommy started to feel comfortable and participate to all activities at school exhibiting a unique intelligence.

Tommy was the one who informed Isabel about Tina. They lived in the same street in Bethnal Green.

'Ms Pearlbrooke, there is this girl living with her grandmother just two houses away from mine. Her grandmother is very sick and I used to share my food with her. Now that I am away, she will have no one,' he said, and his eyes filled with tears.

'Let's go and find her,' Isabel said immediately, and Tommy wiped his tears away. They went to the kitchen together and prepared a basket with foods of all kinds and then, Tommy dived into the armoire where Isabel kept all the donated clothes to find something to fit his young friend. When they arrived outside her house Isabel noticed how Tommy refused to even glimpse in the direction of his own though it was only two doors away. They knocked on Tina's door and waited patiently.

'Tina, it's me Tommy,' he said in a low voice.

The door immediately opened slowly with a creak and

the girl looked outside; her eyes wide open, quite startled.

'Tommy! You came back!' she exclaimed, and Tommy shushed her.

'Be quiet! I don't want them to know I am here,' he said nodding in the direction of his house.

Tina then looked at Isabel.

'You have come with an angel,' she chirped. 'I knew you would come. My nanna told me so, just before she closed her eyes to sleep… forever,' she said and sniffled.

'Your nanna died?' Tommy asked and hugged Tina. 'When?'

'I am not sure how long ago. Some days,' Tina said and held tightly onto Tommy's hand. 'I was alone and so scared,' she said.

'I am sorry Tina. I didn't know. Ms Pearlbrooke we can't leave Tina alone here.'

Isabel fell to her knees and caressed the little girl's hair.

'How old are you, my little fairy?'

'I am five, I think mam.'

'Where are your parents, my love?'

Tina raised both her shoulders.

'I have no one. I only had my nanna.'

'Please, Ms Pearlbrooke. Let Tina come with us,' Tommy pleaded.

'Come where? Where were you mister?' Tina said, squinting her eyes, putting her hands on her hips. Isabel laughed at the feisty little girl.

'I live in a school now,' Tommy said with pride.

'A school? But girls do not go to school,' Tina said and wiggled her little nose.

'I have a lot of girls in my school. In fact, one of them is the same age as you,' Isabel pointed out enthusiastically.

'You will love it there. It is clean and warm. We have food every day and we learn so many things. You will be safe there… with me,' Tommy explained, and Isabel couldn't help feeling moved hearing this young boy acknowledging her efforts.

Tina didn't wait any longer. She stood between Isabel and Tommy and held their hands. They all three walked away as fast as they could; the two children turning their backs on and, at last, escaping their awful past.

Nathan couldn't help but tear up hearing their story.

'We should write a play about those two,' he suggested.

'But this time the ending will be a happy one,' Isabel insisted and kissed her husband-to-be tenderly and with a smile on his face, he slept tightly immediately after.

Chapter 26

Isabel had just finished writing the last letter addressed to her parents informing them of her news. She was rubbing her neck trying to relax when she heard a knock on the door.

'Come in, Mr Thorns,' Isabel said but when the door opened, she was surprised to see Alistair instead.

'Alistair! What a nice surprise,' Isabel said and got up to welcome him. Alistair reluctantly entered the room.

'I am sorry for the intrusion. Mr Thorns said I would find Nathan in his study,' he said apologetically, playing awkwardly with the brim of his hat.

'Nathan isn't awake yet. I can wake him up if you need to talk to him. We fell asleep late last night,' Isabel admitted with a wide smile. Alistair peered at Isabel's hand.

'Ah, he proposed, and you accepted. I guess I should congratulate you, my lady,' Alistair said but Isabel caught the whiff of disappointment in Alistair's voice. He stood still in the middle of the room. 'I should take my leave, now. There is no point talking to Nathan anymore,' he said.

'Wait!' Isabel exclaimed. 'Obviously there is something

wrong. Let me call Nathan.'

'I don't think anything is going to change. I can't make him see reason and since you have accepted his marriage proposal there is no hope.'

Isabel fought off an ill feeling.

'What's going on, Alistair? Please tell me.'

'Nathan will kill me, but I think you should know. A golden opportunity has arisen. His play, Isabel. His play can travel the world. Our investor, Mr Donahue, has arranged for a tour on the continent and in New York. Nathan Dunkan will become known world-wide!'

'This is extraordinarily good news!' *My God... why didn't he say anything to me?* Isabel wondered still flustered by the great news.

'Donahue refuses to invest his money unless Nathan is in the lead.'

'Quite reasonably I would argue,' Isabel commented and Alistair eyes widened in amazement.

'So, you can see how invaluable this opportunity is.'

'Of course! This is his life's dream,' Isabel argued. 'Does Nathan object?'

'He does. He refuses to join the tour because…' Alistair hesitated for a second.

'Because?' Isabel asked in all agony.

'Because of you. And the children, he said. He got into a huge fight with Donahue. He refused to listen to me, to anyone. He is risking all we have worked for,' Alistair snarled quite frustrated.

Isabel couldn't believe it. Nathan was throwing away a golden opportunity.

'How long is the tour for?' She asked the dreaded question.

'A year.'

Isabel stomach squeezed to the news. Nathan would have to be away from her for a whole year but the price she would have to pay was small compared to the benefit.

'A year is a long time, but I am not going anywhere. I will wait for him for as long as is needed. He must know that,' Isabel uttered.

'This is exactly what I told him too. But he said he can't be away from you. He said he… needs you,' Alistair intoned and, as if in disbelief, raised both his hands over his head.

Isabel couldn't believe it. Nathan loved her so much that he was prepared to abandon his dream. The timing was not ideal but still she couldn't allow him to make any more sacrifices for her. She had to talk some sense into him and fast.

'When are you leaving?' Isabel asked

'We were departing on the 27th of July, but I don't know any more than that.'

'The 27th?' Isabel exclaimed. 'This is an omen.'

'Omen? What is it about this date? Nathan was flabbergasted too,' Alistair asked. The expiration of their contract was going to be the beginning of Nathan's new phase in life. *This can't be a coincidence.* Isabel had to set him free. She would miss Nathan tremendously, but she couldn't stand in his way, he had to pursue his dream.

Nathan was still fast asleep when Isabel went back into their bedroom. She couldn't bring herself to wake him. She just wanted to take a few moments to gaze at him while lying in their bed, to keep this image in her heart and mind, to cherish it for all the time they were going to be apart. She was determined to persuade Nathan to take this wonderful opportunity, though it pained her immensely knowing that they would be apart for a whole year.

'Nathan, my love,' she softly called him while caressing his soft hair and then kissed him on his chest. Nathan woke and instinctively reached out to put his arms around her. He pulled her closer to his bare body and held her tight before he opened his eyes. The warmth of his body next to hers made her feel safe and blissful and yet, she was about to deny herself for a year. He leaned in further and kissed her passionately, her lips and her throat, lower down to her chest.

'My love we need to talk,' she said softly but her little moan only encouraged Nathan to continue kissing her.

'We will,' he said. 'Right after I am done making love to you,' he said in a husky voice that sent shivers down her spine.

'Alistair was here,' Isabel blurted. Nathan stopped and looked at her with furrowed eyebrows.

'I don't want to talk to him. Please send him away and come back to our bed.'

'He is already gone. I promised I would talk to you since you refuse to listen to him,' Isabel said. Nathan jumped out the bed. He covered his eyes with his hands trying to steady his breathing.

'Did he tell you?' he asked.

'He did.'

'He had no right,' Nathan bellowed.

'Don't be mad at him, my love. He only wants what's best for you,' Isabel offered, and Nathan chuckled.

'He only wants what is best for him. He craves for fame.'

'As you should too,' Isabel advised him. 'Your play is going to travel the world. You will be famous well beyond the London boarders. This is your life's dream, Nathan.'

'YOU are my life!' Nathan protested. 'All I want, Isabel, is what we were planning last night. A warm household with you, Tina and Tommy. I want our life in the countryside. I want to wake up every morning next to you, feel your body, kiss you, create with you. I need you. Can't you see?'

Nathan's outburst shook Isabel to the core. This man loved her truly but still she had to make him see reason.

'We will have all these moments, my love. I promise you. Only it will take us a little longer to get there. I will wait for you, always. Please, Nathan. This is important. Please, as a personal favour. You will be a playwright of great renown. I know it deep in my heart. Do not sacrifice this for me.'

'You have got it all wrong, Isabel. I am not willing to sacrifice my family for fame. I do not need it anymore. We have fortune, we have our health, our children. We have planned a beautiful life together. I don't need anything else.'

Isabel could see that she had to take a different approach to persuade him though secretly deep inside, every word escaping her mouth, pained her. Making this decision was conflicting; should she listen to her head or her heart? Her heart had scalded her before. She had to find a way to get through to him. Make him see sense.

'What if we joined too?' she suggested enthusiastically, while inside her heart was breaking at the thought of his leaving her and the children, leaving the life they had promised to live together. 'Not right away and not for the whole tour but we could come and find you and spend some time all together abroad.'

Nathan's mien started to relax a little. That idea seemed to agree with him.

'Is this even possible?' he asked.

'I will need some time to reorganise the running of the school, and I was thinking of finishing decorating the house but right after, in two or three months, we could join you in Europe. Especially in Paris. It would be lovely for the children to visit that beautiful city. Thalia can teach them so many wonderful things.'

'We are definitely spending time in Paris,' Nathan muttered, rubbing his chin obviously starting to warm to the idea. 'If I recall correctly, we will be arriving there mid-October and spending about a month performing the play,' Nathan said, and Isabel rejoiced.

'This is wonderful. The timing works perfectly.'

'And after that?' Nathan asked with a raised eyebrow.

'After that we will return to London and wait for you to come back to us.'

'That will be a torture,' Nathan argued and exhaled quite frustrated. 'We will have to be married before I leave,' he said.

'That can be arranged. We have a whole month ahead of us.'

'And we will talk to Tommy and Tina.'

'We can do that today,' Isabel said encouragingly trying to veil her growing sadness realising that Nathan was really going on tour. *It has to be done,* she repeated, an affirmation to herself. It was Nathan's destiny to be on that tour. All the signs were there.

'And our contract!' Nathan exclaimed startling Isabel. 'I would like to burn it,' he said, and Isabel laughed heartily.

'By all means, my love.'

Chapter 27

Isabel was quite nervous when she walked through the door of her house that morning with Nathan on her side. It was such an important day for her, for her future. That very morning, she was committing her whole life to two innocent souls. Maybe it was different for mothers bearing their own children. Maybe they had time to prepare, and their maternal instincts guided them as to what to do. She couldn't help but wonder whether she would make a good mother, if she had the qualities and virtues required. Nathan squeezed her hand tightly.

'We can do this,' he said and smiled encouragingly at Isabel.

They found all the children in the drawing room which was temporarily turned into a classroom. Ms Cabbage was teaching them geography.

'Who can tell me where we are on the map? Ms Cabbage asked and both Tommy and Nigel raised their hands. 'Nigel, come to the front and show us.' Ms Cabbage invited him to her side to point to the map that was laid on the round table.

'We are here,' Nigel answered but Sally's giggles tipped him of his mistake. He frowned and stepped back crossing his hands in front of his chest. 'If you are so smart, why don't you show us where we are?'

'We are over here,' Sally said, pointing correctly at England on the map. 'You were pointing at Italy.'

'Italy looks like a boot,' Tina remarked evoking the laughter of all the children. 'I would love to go there one day,' she said. Isabel and Nathan looked at each other and nodded knowingly.

'Ms Pearlbrooke, Mr Dunkan! We didn't hear you coming in,' Ms Cabbage said finally noticing them and all the children turned in their direction. Tina ran to Isabel and hugged her tight. Isabel picked her up and gave her a little peck on the cheek. *I must be already doing something correctly,* she thought, and her heart filled with hope.

'Children, please sit down. I have some news that I would like to share with you,' Isabel said. She patiently waited for everyone to sit on the floor again and to quieten. She cleared her throat and continued.

'First, I would like you to know that our school is almost ready. You will be going back in two weeks' time,' Isabel announced and all the children cheered. 'Our school is going to be even better than what it used to be. The classroom is bigger, and we have a surprise for you. We are building a small stage in our parlour for your drama lessons.'

The children clapped to the news and chattered with excitement.

'Now, we have some more news,' Nathan continued. 'Ms Pearlbrooke and I are betrothed. Our wedding is in four weeks, and you are all invited.'

The news of the betrothal caused even more excited commotion. There were claps and cheers and Ms

Cabbage trotted across the room with open arms to hug and congratulate them both with tears in her eyes.

'This is the best day!' Theo exclaimed. 'We are invited to a wedding. I have never been to a wedding before. There will be plenty of food, will there not?' he asked

'Of course. And we are ordering an enormous cake,' Nathan answered, and Theo's eyes grew huge and he licked his lips.

'Are we going to dance? Mary asked.

'Yes, there is going to be some dancing too,' Isabel explained.

'But we don't know any dances,' Sally remarked, placing her palm to her cheek.

'You don't? I am going to rectify this oversight at once,' Isabel promised. 'Ms Cabbage, as of tomorrow I am hiring a dance instructor to teach the children how to dance.'

For the next hour the children bombarded Isabel and Nathan with questions about their wedding and their new school and when they finally calmed Isabel called Tommy and Tina to follow them for a private talk. They all four walked into Isabel's study. The two children looked at each other wondering, worried frowns across their brows, eyes shifting around the room, unable to settle on anything for too long. Tina eventually looked at Tommy and shook her head at him as if trying to instil some calm in them both. He shrugged his shoulders with a quiet sigh, but he continued to fidget on his feet. Isabel's hands trembled with agony. Nathan, however, seemed a lot more confident and nodded encouragingly at Isabel. They invited the two children to sit on the newly arrived settee.

'Tommy and Tina, Nathan and I invited you here

because we wanted to discuss something with you.'

'Are you sending us away?' Tommy asked in a trembling voice, his eyes wide, his cheeks suddenly rosy from the heat rising with the evident panic within him

'Don't be silly, Tommy,' Tina scolded him. 'Ms Pearlbrooke would never abandon us,' she said and gave him a little punch on the shoulder.

'That is true, Tommy. I would never send you away. You can stay with us for as long as you like. In fact, Nathan and I were hoping…' she tried to continue but strong emotions overwhelmed her. Nathan held her hand and continued.

'We were hoping that you would allow us to care and provide for you for life. To become your family,' he said, and Isabel noticed how he too teared, but he managed to maintain his equanimity and smiled at the two children who were left gawking at them, their mouths dropped open.

The first to speak was Tina.

'Do you mean that you would like to become our parents?' she asked, and Isabel nodded emphatically unable to hold her tears back anymore.

'Yes. That is what we are asking you. Would you allow us to care and provide for you? To become your parents? There is nothing in this world that would make us happier,' Isabel said, drying her tears.

Tina leapt to her feet and rushed to Isabel's lap. She hugged her tightly and kissed her on the cheek again and again. She, then, slid off and jumped onto Nathan's lap. She hugged him tightly too.

'Thank you, thank you! I will have the most beautiful mother and father!' Tina exclaimed. She wriggled out of

Nathan's embrace and rushed to Tommy.

'We're going to be brother and sister. Tommy, do you hear?' She started pulling his sleeve. 'Come on Tommy. Please smile. Why are you sad? Don't you want me as your sister?'

Tommy didn't answer. He stood still looking at Isabel and Nathan seeming pensive.

'What is it Tommy?' Nathan asked.

'You do not have to accept our offer,' Isabel explained. 'You don't have to come and live with us. You can still stay at our school, continue to learn and be cared for there.'

Tommy's eyes filled with tears. He hid his face behind his hands and Isabel rushed to his side. She hugged him and kissed him tenderly.

'Everything is going to be alright,' she whispered to him.

'No, it is not!' Tommy exclaimed. 'Tina is lucky. She doesn't have any parents. But what if my parents come to get me. I don't want to go with them. I want to stay with you. I am afraid, I am so afraid,' he cried out. Isabel and Tina both wrapped their arms around him.

'Listen to me Tommy. We will never give you up. You will never return to Bethnal Green. We will fight for you to stay with us, and to keep you safe always,' Nathan affirmed.

Isabel explained how they were moving to Witney and Nathan described to them in detail his estate, the vast forest and the small community with the nicest people. He told them funny stories of his childhood and promised them that they would have the best of time there. They were going to build good, happy memories and share many happy times together as a family.

'Are we ever coming back to London? I want to see my friends,' Tina insisted.

'Of course we are. I will have to be here often to support Ms Cabbage and the school,' said Isabel.

'I won't come back ever,' Tommy said determinedly. 'I want to stay with Nathan in Witney. Can I please?'

'You can, but I should warn you that we will be moving there in a year's time,' Nathan answered. 'I have to be away for a while. I'm travelling across Europe and then to New York with my theatre company.'

'But the exciting news is that we will go visit Nathan abroad too,' Isabel added.

'We are?' Tommy asked in wonderment.

'How would you feel if we went to Paris,' Isabel suggested.

'And Italy! I would love to go to a country that looks like a boot,' Tina said.

All four stayed in the study for hours, talking and making plans for their future. They only stopped when their stomachs started growling with hunger. Isabel was beyond happy. That day her dreams came true.

'One more question, can I call you Mother and Father?' Tina asked as they were exiting the study. Isabel's heart melted; blessed and happy. She never believed she would hear the words.

Chapter 28

'White. Isabel's wedding dress should be white,' Catherine insisted. She picked up a bolt of silk fabric. 'Hold this please,' she ordered and placed it across Isabel's outstretched forearms.

'I think this silver fabric is the ideal colour for Isabel,' Lydia said and, she too, placed a bolt on top.

'I disagree with both of you!' Diana exclaimed. 'Isabel's colour is light blue,' she insisted and stacked one more bolt of fabric on Isabel's forearms who was now struggling to hold them all at once. 'I think she should forget about the wedding and join a circus. Look how skilled she is balancing the bolts,' Diana jested and the four women started laughing.

'I wonder if you, ladies, will ever agree to anything,' Isabel said, gazing at herself in a mirror trying to decide on one of their suggested colours.

'We all agree that your husband-to-be is divine,' Catherine said and winked at Isabel.

Isabel smiled thinking of her handsome husband and all the naughty things he had done to her that morning. She blushed profusely and unfortunately it didn't go unnoticed.

'Should we dare to ask what you were just thinking about?' Lydia asked cheekily.

'I would never reveal anything. Besides, Diana is still unmarried. I would not like to be responsible for the innocent's corruption,' Isabel proclaimed.

'You may need to tell me soon,' Diana blurted.

'Excuse me? Are you flirting with a beau my dear sister? Why am I not aware of that?' Catherine said slightly irritated.

'I can't reveal anything yet. It is something unexpected and quite recent. I am not even certain he is interested. I like him a lot but…' Diana confessed.

'Tell us. We may be able to help,' Lydia offered.

'Oh no, no! I don't need your help. Especially you my dear sister-in-law. You will not meddle. At least not until I am certain beyond doubt that I really like the man.'

'Where did you meet? Surely you can tell us as much,' Catherine asked.

'I cannot say.'

'Leave her alone. She will tell us when she is ready,' Isabel said and discreetly she turned to Diana and mouthed under her breath *you are telling me*. But Diana pretended she didn't see her.

'On another topic. Did you realise what a hubbub Isabel's wedding announcement caused?' Diana mentioned. 'Nathan Dunkan, the famous actor is the wealthy Baron of Witney. How did he manage to keep that a secret for so long?'

'Women were chasing him just for being a handsome actor. Can you imagine what would have happened if they knew he was titled and rich?' Isabel explained. 'The ton mamas would have been after him relentlessly,' Isabel commented and the three ladies agreed. 'I am wearing white with this lace for the trim,' Isabel decided.

'Excellent choice madame,' the modiste said.

'And we will need a smaller size dress of the same fabric for my daughter,' Isabel requested, and her heart filled with happiness. *My daughter,* words she never imagined she would be blessed to utter.

'Are the children happy?' Catherine asked.

'Deliriously happy. Tina is already calling us Mother and Father. Tommy is not addressing as such yet, but I understand. It is all so new to him and he is still scared that his parents may claim him back. He can't wait for us to move to Witney. Quite frankly, I long for it, too. Being close to nature and spending my time reading books and enjoying the quietness is all I have ever secretly wished for. Nathan is going to focus on his writing, and he is going to take on some of the managing responsibilities of his estate. It will be good for Tommy to experience it since he is very likely to inherit the baronet one day. However, I suspect he is particularly interested in performing arts. He insists on going to the theatre to see Nathan perform almost every day. He loves it.'

'From the slums of Bethnal Green to inheriting a baronet. He is such a lucky little boy,' Diana suggested. 'But when you move to the country, we will miss you so much.'

'We still have plenty of time together. We are moving in a year's time as soon as Nathan returns from his tour. But once we settle, you should visit us. Nathan says his estate is beautiful. There is a vast forest surrounding it with long green fields beyond and spectacular views from every part of the home.'

'John would enjoy that immensely. We haven't been to the country for such a long time, and he misses it so much. We went to Nottinghamshire a few years ago to inspect our properties there but the memories devastated me,' Lydia said, and tears welled up in her eyes.

'You miss Oscar, don't you?' Catherine asked and held her hand tightly.

'I do. He was my best friend. I admit that time healed the wounds and all that is left is the love I once felt for him,' Lydia admitted. 'I miss the countryside, riding my horses without any care in the world. Riding in Hyde Park is a very poor alternative. And now I cannot do this either,' Lydia exhaled exasperated.

'Because of the …' Catherine said and with her eyes she pointed to Lydia's tummy.

' Shh! Yes. We can't announce it yet. It is too soon.'

'Another baby. You are so blessed,' Isabel whispered with a wide smile.

'I am too old. I don't know how this happened again,' Lydia said with a frown.

'Do we need to have the talk about baby making?' Catherine jested.

'Yes, please,' Diana urged her.

'Diana!' Catherine scolded her and all of them burst into laughter.

'You two will never change,' Isabel commented.

Chapter 29

Happiness and sadness all became mixed together. Isabel and Nathan were getting more and more desperate for each other as the time of Nathan's departure approached but at the same time their wedding day, on the 26th of July, was giving them so much joy. The day before their wedding they decided to stay in their bed not leaving each other for a second. All they wanted to do was make love, read books together and talk about their future, make beautiful plans and comfort each other when they felt sorrowful for the time they would be spending apart.

Their wedding day was a celebration of love. Everybody who truly cared for the couple was there. Isabel's parents, Catherine, Diana and Lydia, Thalia and her husband who travelled from Paris to rejoice in the happy event, Mr Thorns and Ms Cabbage, all the children of the school who were beautifully dressed and had combed their hair meticulously, Nathan's sister with her family and all the cast members from Nathan's play.

Isabel, blissfully happy, could see them all while standing at the edge of the aisle on Nathan's side. But the sight of Tommy in his double-breasted suit jacket and shirt, finely ruffled along the front opening, and Tina in her white lace dress frilled from the waist down, waiting for them at the altar at the other end of the aisle, made her heart beat fast. She was going to burst with joy.

'You are so beautiful. I love you,' Nathan whispered in her ear and held her hand in his, tightly, as they walked down the aisle.

The aahs and oohs of the guests were cloaked by the uncontrollable whimpers of Catherine. Isabel looked at her wondering about her reaction and Catherine signed back not to mind her while her husband, Thomas, was doing his best to comfort her. Her friend loved her; Isabel knew it well and Catherine's tears were of great joy. Isabel felt blessed for her friends. They had been supporting and protecting her all those years asking for nothing in return.

The ceremony was beautiful, and peace surrounded Isabel. She had finally had everything she needed in her life, and she was grateful for Nathan who had not given up on her. The words of the priest were not simply uniting a husband and wife but bonding their whole family and at the end of the sermon, all four of them, Nathan, Isabel, Tommy and Tina hugged each other.

For the wedding breakfast, they were all invited back to Nathan's town house. Isabel had managed to finish the refurbishment of the dining room. The room, now bathed in peach blossom on the walls and maroon curtains at the windows, showed off its grandeur. There were no family portraits on the walls yet, but Isabel planned to commission an artist to paint theirs as soon as Nathan returned from his tour. There was only one portrait in the alcove over an impressive mahogany sideboard. That of Nathan's parents. Beautiful floral installations of pink

Bougainvillea took pride of place on the grand dining table. The great variety of pastries, from rolls to pies, the eggs and ham and the huge cake on the table caused a lot of excitement as the children hovered around the table eyeballing the treats, licking their lips and rubbing their tummies

'I am starting with a huge piece of cake,' Theo announced.

'I am having cherry pie and some eggs,' Nigel said, rubbing his hands. 'Can we, Ms Pearlbrooke?'

'You can have as much food as you want,' Isabel said, and she caressed their little heads tenderly.

'My love, I would like to introduce to you my sister, Carolina,' Nathan said.

'I am so happy to finally make your acquaintance,' Isabel said gleefully. Carolina was a short plump woman who did not share much resemblance with her brother apart from her green eyes. Her mien exerted kindness and Isabel felt instantly close to her.

'Boys wait!' Nathan exclaimed with urgency. Theo was halfway up the table with Nigel pushing him in a desperate effort to reach the cake. 'Excuse me for a second,' Nathan said and rushed to the boys to avert the destruction that was lurking.

'I am so happy to have a sister. Nathan, wrote to me that you are beautiful, and I can see why my brother fell so much in love with you,' Carolina said and hugged Isabel. 'I can't wait for you to move to Witney. My children will have their cousins to play with and I promise I will help you with the newborn coming,' she added in a conspiring lowered voice.

Isabel's mouth dropped and she looked at Carolina with

raised eyebrows quite perplexed. 'But I am not…'

'Oh no! Do not think that Nathan revealed your secret. He didn't say a word to me. I just have a nose for these things,' she claimed, pointing at her wriggling nose. 'I better go help my brother with the two little menaces over there. You are the bride, and you should get some rest,' she added and winked at her. She fled to Nathan and the boys who were trying unsuccessfully to cut the cake and were making a terrible mess all around.

Whatever did she mean? Isabel thought, standing speechless in the middle of the room.

'Congratulations!' Isabel heard in a chorus of voices that brought her back from her thoughts. It was Catherine and Diana.

'What is the matter?' Catherine asked.

'I think that my sister-in-law just called me fat,' Isabel said quite amazed.

'Excuse me?' Catherine asked.

'She insinuated I am with child. She is not aware, of course, but you know well that this is not possible. Have I gained weight?' Isabel asked and ran her hands over her tummy, her thighs.

'Well…' Diana offered, and Isabel's eyes opened wide.

'Diana!' Catherine scolded her and nudged her in the ribs.

'So, it is true,' Isabel cried out.

'Your breasts look bigger. Look at your bustline. Your dress is going to erupt,' Diana blurted and Catherine placed her hand on her forehand, shaking her head in resentment.

'Diana,' she said disheartened.

'I don't think my breasts are any bigger. The modiste just got the measurement wrong. I realised when the dress was delivered to me but there was no time to amend it. That is all,' Isabel protested and looked down at her breasts again. She made a mental note to ask Nathan. If anyone knew her body better than herself it was him. She decided to forget about her sister-in-law's inappropriate remark and enjoy herself. The musicians she had hired were now playing a Waltz and she longed to dance with her husband having missed the chance at the last ball they had attended together.

'Husband, dance with me,' she said, and Nathan followed her to the middle of the room where the children had already started dancing in threes and fours exhibiting some of their newly acquired dancing skills. Isabel was quite impressed.

'Are you happy, my love?' Nathan asked.

'Deliriously,' Isabel said and smiled back at him.

'I can't wait for this to finish and be alone with you,' Nathan whispered in her ear and Isabel face flushed with heat at the thought of them being together in bed.

'We should first show Tina and Tommy the surprise we have for them,' Isabel reminded Nathan.

'Let's do that right now. We don't have to wait for the guests to leave.'

Isabel agreed. She was too excited to wait any longer. They asked Tina and Tommy to follow them upstairs and when they stood in front of the two closed doors Isabel realised her nerves were crashing in on her. She really hoped the children liked what she and Nathan had prepared for them.

'Isabel and I have a surprise for you,' Nathan announced in excitement as well. With a flurry he turned the handles of both doors and they flew open to reveal two beautifully decorated children's rooms.

The two children stood still, unable to utter a word. They looked at each other and then faced Isabel and Nathan.

'Mother, is this my room?' Tina asked first pointing at the room with pink walls and light green upholstery. Isabel nodded yes unable to utter a word such was the agony of seeing her daughter so overwhelmed with delight.

Tina ran inside and she, then, stopped.

'Look, Tommy, my bed is huge, and I have a mirror and a table with combs and brushes and a perfume bottle. And a dolls house!' she exclaimed. She ran out again and threw herself into Nathan's embrace. 'Thank you, thank you so much,' she said and started jumping up and down. 'Tommy! Don't you just stand there dawdling. Let's go to your room,' Tina said and pulled him by the hand into his light blue room. 'Wow, your bed is even bigger. Look, you have so many books and little wooden soldiers. And you too have a mirror and a comb. Finally, no excuses any more for your fuzzy hair. You will have to comb it every day now,' Tina tweeted on happily while Tommy stood silently in the middle of the room, gazing at everything in disbelief. Isabel walked to his side and caressed his back.

'Do you like it, Tommy?'

'Is this… mine?' he asked in disbelief.

'Yes,' Nathan added, and he also placed his hand on the boy's shoulder, tapping it lightly. 'You are our children. You will stay with us from now on. And Tommy, I trust you will care for the girls now that I am going to be away.'

Tommy turned round and hugged both Isabel and Nathan stretching his arms around them, trying to encircle them in his embrace.

'I always dreamt of this, but I never believed it could

come true. Thank you so much. I promise I will take care of Tina and Isabel with all my might,' Tommy said with tears in his eyes. 'But Nathan please hurry back,' he added and Isabel felt his words like a sharp double-bladed knife piercing her gut. Tommy was hurting too by Nathan's imminent departure.

'Mother, can I show my room to Rosy, please?'

'Of course you can,' Isabel said and before she even finished her sentence Tina was already descending the stairs to go fetch her friend.

'How about you Tommy? Would you like to call any of your friends to come and join you upstairs? Nathan asked.

'Not today if you don't mind. I would like to spend some time alone in my room,' Tommy answered.

This was the perfect end to a perfect day, Isabel thought thinking back to the happiness of her children. But then, she thought of Nathan's departure the next day and nausea smothered her.

Chapter 30

The dreaded day had come. Isabel and Nathan had woken up early in the morning to break their fast with their children. Mr Thorns joined them too. They all chattered happily remembering the events of the wedding day, but Isabel still nauseous was trying hard not to burst into tears. She had to be strong for Nathan and her children, but she wanted to crawl back into her bed and stay there. She was aware how important this tour was for Nathan's ongoing fame and success but at the same time she wished she had been more selfish and hadn't persuaded her husband to leave them. If anyone was to blame for her misery, it was solely her.

When the time came for Nathan to leave, they rose from the table and said their goodbyes. Isabel's knees threatened to buckle under her and she had to push herself hard to stand up and follow her husband to the waiting carriage. Nathan hugged and kissed the children and then, he stepped outside with Isabel. They held onto each other tightly.

'You are trembling,' Nathan observed.

'I am going to miss you,' Isabel said with tears welling up her eyes, unable to conceal her sorrow anymore.

'I hate this. I don't want to go. I will talk to Donahue again. I know plenty of actors who would jump at the opportunity,' Nathan said.

'And let someone else have the glory after all your hard work?' Isabel reminded him.

'I am only going because you promised me you will meet me with the children in Paris. And I am determined not to travel to New York. I am not leaving you for that long. It is an impossible thought,' Nathan protested.

Isabel could not debate Nathan on the matter anymore. She held tightly onto him, mostly because she had to steady herself. She couldn't feel her legs, her eyes were darkening and everything had started spinning around her. She was not well but she didn't want to confess her ill-health to Nathan. She was certain that her sadness had weakened her or maybe she was coming down with something. She realised that she had to let him go and rush to her bed.

'My love, it is time. Alistair is waiting for you in the carriage,' she managed to say, and they broke their embrace, pulling away from him hurt her immensely.

'He wanted to make sure I didn't escape,' Nathan commented, and he chuckled motioning to Alistair who was staring at them through the carriage window.

'Go now, I can't endure this any longer,' she urged him and fought to give him a smile. She turned her back on him and walked inside hurryingly. Wobbling, she managed to reach the staircase, but her legs gave up on her. She sat down clumsily on the bottom step, trying to catch her breath but she felt her brain shutting down. She was cognisant to understand that Tina and Tommy were next to her, calling her name and screaming for help. And as she was losing consciousness, she discerned Tommy's figure running out the front door. She tried to call him back, but her voice failed her.

Nathan had been fighting a nasty feeling all morning. Something didn't feel right. His logic and his instincts conflicted with each other and if he had learnt something in life it was to trust his instincts. He wiggled uncomfortably on the carriage seat.

'You are doing the right thing,' Alistair intoned.

'Something doesn't feel right. Isabel was not her usual self. I have never seen her so fragile before,' Nathan said and swallowed hard.

'It is understandable, she is unhappy to see you leaving, especially so soon after your wedding,' Alistair offered.

'It was not just that. Isabel is the strongest woman I have ever met in my life. She has been through so much. Her school burned down and her strength, her resolve, her tenacity, in dealing with the situation humbled me. Today, it is something different,' he said, and his stomach tightened into a knot.

'Or you are just imagining things just because you want to go back to her,' Alistair said with furrowed eyebrows.

Father! Nathan jumped in his seat.

'Did you hear that?' he asked Alistair.

'Hear what?'

'I think I heard Tommy calling me,' Nathan said and looked outside the window.

'I didn't hear anything. That confirms my theory that you are imagining things,' Alistair scolded him.

Nathan sat back dropping his head. Alistair was probably right. Besides, Tommy didn't call him Father yet, he said to himself to justify what now felt like a vile premonition. The sudden screams of the driver and the abrupt halt of the carriage shook Nathan and Alistair who both nearly fell of their seats. It took them a few seconds to realise what had happened and Nathan noticed how people were running past their carriage. He stood up and flung open the door to see what the commotion was about. The carriage driver was frantically shouting.

'He just jumped in front of the carriage!'

Some women were fanning themselves and a couple were crying.

'Is he alive?' Nathan heard in the crowd's mumbles. Nathan jumped from the carriage and moved forward. A lot of people were standing in front of their carriage, blocking the road and the driver, pale faced, was craning his neck trying to see, trembling and wiping his sweaty face with his handkerchief.

'What is going on?' Nathan asked, his voice cracking as his gut feeling was warning him of eminent danger.

'A little boy jumped in front of our carriage. I tried… I tried to stop but I am not certain… the horses may have stomped…' the driver muttered.

Nathan, alarmed, ran to the gathered crowed and made way to reach the little boy. It was Tommy, there lying on the ground, his face dusted with debris, his closed eyes and once glowing cheeks already bruised. Nathan in agony fell on his knees.

'This is my son! Tommy, Tommy, can you hear me?' Nathan screamed and then, quickly composing himself, he examined the rest of Tommy's body for cuts and bruises. He couldn't see any and he started feeling hopeful. 'Tommy, open your eyes,' he shouted and kissed his forehead. Tommy opened his eyes and squinted.

'Father?' he repeated and Nathan's heart almost broke with the sheer happiness and relief. His boy had come around and called him Father. He pulled him into his arms and filled his face with kisses.

'The boy is alive!' someone exclaimed.

'Why Tommy? Why did you jump in front of the carriage?' Nathan asked tenderly.

Tommy then opened his eyes wide and weakly pushed himself up from the ground.

'Mother. She is unwell,' he said and grabbed Nathan's hand. 'We need to go to her,' Tommy said and he pulled Nathan as hard as his dwindling energy could

Nathan lost his breath with the news. His instincts had warned him. He knew he had been right all along.

'Let's go,' he said, and he swooped Tommy up into his arms and started running back towards the house, ignoring Alistair whose shouting was dimming with every stride he took away from the carriage.

When they reached home Nathan was sweaty and dusty. He almost brought the door down with his banging. One more second and he was determined to break it down. Mr Thorns answered and though quite startled said, 'Isabel is in bed. The doctor is with her,' and before he even finished his phrase Nathan was climbing the staircase two steps at a time. He didn't knock on their bedroom door. He burst inside unable to contain himself. He was about to lose his mind. When he stepped inside, Isabel was on the bed crying and Tina was lying across her, pressing her ear against her tummy. The doctor was standing, putting his stethoscope in his bag. Isabel's eyes grew huge when she saw Nathan and her hand shot in front of her mouth. Tina disentangled herself from her mother and stepped away from the bed.

'Father?' she said with a wide smile. 'You are back!' she squealed.

'Sir, congratulations are in order,' The doctor said, and Nathan looked between him and Isabel in wonderment, trying to understand.

'Nothing to worry about. Your wife is in perfect health. She was lucky she didn't injure herself with the fall on the stairs. I reassure you the baby is safe,' the doctor continued, and Nathan's eyes filled with tears realising what the doctor was saying.

'We are having a baby?' Nathan asked, looking at Isabel and Isabel nodded with a bright, wide smile which reached her ears.

'Your wife explained to me the assumed difficulties due to the injury of the past. It would certainly have been hard for her to conceive but I have seen it happen this way before. I am only going to ask you to be very careful from now on. Take long rests, eat well but I would also recommend going out for a short leisurely walk once a day if possible. Some exercise is imperative and, in my observation, it facilitates the labour as well. Mrs Dunkan, if you feel any discomfort please call me immediately,' the doctor added and left the room.

Nathan walked towards Isabel and sat beside her. He pulled her close and caressed her face. He kissed her tenderly on the lips being careful not to make any sudden moves.

'I am not going to break, Nathan,' Isabel said and kissed him again. 'Why are you here and why are you two all dusty?' Isabel asked examining both Nathan and Tommy from head to toe with a raised eyebrow. Tommy looked worryingly at Nathan.

'Tommy came all the way to the theatre to find me. When he told me you were unwell, we just started running back home. It didn't occur to me to call for a carriage. I lost my mind with the worry, of not knowing what had happened to you.'

Isabel did not seem convinced, but Nathan was not going to reveal to her that Tommy had jumped in front of his carriage to stop it. She would be too upset, but he was going to have a talk with his boy later that day.

'Your tour?' Isabel asked Nathan.

'My tour? You can protest all you want Wife, but I am not going anywhere,' Nathan told her decisively. 'Now, you need to rest. Tommy and I will clean up and I have to take care of a few matters,' Nathan said.

As Nathan left his wife to rest, he noticed Tommy's gloominess while Tina was happy, dancing to a tune she was singing to herself.

'We are having a baby,' she said. 'Father, I promise I will take care of the baby. I will practise with my dolls and learn how to put her to sleep and feed her,' Tina said.

'Her? How can you be so certain?' Nathan asked quite amused.

'I just want a baby sister. I forgot to tell mother. She should know about that so she can tell the baby to be a girl,' Tina said, and Nathan chuckled.

'This isn't how it works, Tina. God decides if we are having a boy or a girl, as He has decided to send us this baby,' Nathan said, and again noticed how Tommy still seemed lost in his thoughts. They all three walked up the stairs to the top of the house and Tina ran to her bedroom to start her mummy practise. Nathan followed Tommy inside his bedroom.

'Tommy, are you feeling unwell? Is your head hurting? Are you may be hurt elsewhere?'

'Please, don't tell Isabel about today,' Tommy pleaded and Nathan didn't miss how he reverted to first-name basis.

'I will not. I wouldn't like to upset your mother. But why did you jump in front of the carriage? It was so risky, Tommy, my boy. We could have lost you,' Nathan said trying to keep calm.

'I was calling you, but you couldn't hear me. The streets were too noisy, and I couldn't think of any other solution. I ran very fast, and I was well ahead of the carriage. I stepped in the middle of the road signalling him to stop but I now believe he might have been short-sighted. He only noticed me when he was too close,' Tommy confessed.

'I beg you, my boy! Please don't you try anything like that again,' Nathan pleaded.

'Nathan, if I may ask. Now that Isabel and you are having your own baby...' Tommy started saying but Nathan stopped him.

'Nothing has changed, Tommy. You and Tina are our children, and you will always be our children, unless you decide differently,' Nathan reassured him.

Tommy fell into his arms.

'Thank you,' he whispered.

Chapter 31

Nathan was free at last. He felt as if a huge burden had been lifted from his shoulders and he cheerfully went to find his wife who, he hoped, was still in bed, following the doctor's orders. He silently walked inside their chamber, relieved to find her asleep. He debated whether he should wake her; he had so much to tell her. He decided to undress and lie beside her. He started caressing her breasts that were gently heaving up and down, following the peaceful pulse of her breathing. Her nipples immediately hardened to his touch and Nathan lightly caught it in his lips over the soft fabric of her gown. Isabel squirmed but she didn't open her eyes. Nathan then put his lips on her throat and kissed it. Encouraged by her reaction, he moved lower, kissing her chest, her tummy, over her clothes. He lifted her dress exposing her thighs. He ran his lips along the length of one leg, starting with her ankle, then her shin, her knee and her inner thigh moving higher. He stopped, momentarily, to check Isabel's reaction; she bit her lip with a smile, her eyes still closed. He moved higher until his face was just hovering over her sensitive area. He opened her soft folds and run his tongue over her sensitive bud again and again. Isabel squirmed and sighed.

'Get inside me now,' she ordered, and Nathan obeyed but he didn't hurry things along. He penetrated slowly, enjoying the wet warmth of her softness, cherishing the moment, teasing her with every motion. They kissed passionately while making love, deep hungry kisses. And when he sensed Isabel building around him, he shivered in anticipation, with bliss. He called out her name, buried his face into her neck, until he too reached his climax.

'I could wake up like that every day,' Isabel said cheerfully and Nathan laughed.

'I have some great news. I don't have to go on tour anymore. I had a talk with Donahue. I explained the situation to him, and he agreed to have someone replace me.'

'This is fantastic news!' Isabel exclaimed. 'But I somehow find it hard to believe he agreed that easily.'

'I promised him that I am giving him my next play.'

'Your next play?'

'Yes, haven't I told you about it? It's about a stunning witch who stole the heart and mind of a talented playwright and he now has no idea what to write about,' Nathan jested but Isabel's mouth formed a small "o".

'So, you have nothing? We immediately need to start thinking of ideas,' Isabel cried but Nathan's face crackled with laughter .

'Do not worry, my love. My head is full of ideas. And now that I am staying here, I will have the time to sit down and write them. I promised Donahue I would send him the play in five months' time just before the baby is born.'

'I still can't quite believe I am pregnant. Your sister knew. She told me at the wedding reception. And I admit I was a little offended at the time,' Isabel confessed, and

Nathan shook his head.

'My sister is a lovely woman, but she has a hard time keeping her thoughts to herself. I need to discuss this with her.'

'The signs, now that I look back, were there all along. I had missed my menses, and my breasts had become swollen, but I never thought I was pregnant, it was impossible for me to imagine after my diagnosis.'

'I had noticed your breasts too,' Nathan admitted with a sly smile.

'Why didn't you say anything?'

'I thought you had gained a little weight, and I loved it.'

'And now I am going to grow huge,' Isabel said, wrinkling her nose.

'I can't wait,' Nathan said and hugged her tightly.

Epilogue

'Push, Isabel, push!' Catherine directed her holding her hand tightly.

'You are very close,' Lydia said and she squeezed Isabel's hand encouragingly.

'Only this time, can you not scream so much, please? You are scaring me,' Diana said, standing at the far corner of the room facing the wall, she daren't look at Isabel and all she was going through to give birth

'Why are you even in here?' her sister asked exasperated.

'She can stay. She amuses me,' Isabel said and squealed in pain; her face contorted in agony.

'You don't sound very amused,' Diana offered and Isabel laughed despite her trauma.

'One more time, my lady,' the doctor said. 'I can see the top of the baby's head.'

'Dear God! All these hours just to see the top of the baby's head,' Diana cried out. 'Come, Isabel. Hurry, please. I can't take this torture any longer. Your walls are lovely, but I can't spend any more time looking at them. You don't even have a nice portrait or a painting to gaze at in here.'

'I apologise for my oversight,' Isabel shouted and

screamed as she was giving it one more push.

'Her torture,' Lydia remarked with a chuckle. 'You have no idea.'

'Catherine didn't take that long. She had the baby in no time.'

'Catherine almost gave birth in a carriage,' Lydia said. 'Thank God, for Michael. He was amazing that day getting you home on time and calling the doctor.' Isabel stopped pushing and looked at Lydia with wide eyes. Catherine also gazed at her in shock. 'Why do you look so shocked? I didn't say anything untrue. If it weren't for Michael, you would have given birth on the sidewalk. He was a hero. You should have named your child after him.'

'I don't believe Thomas would have accepted that gracefully.'

'One more push, Ms Dunkan. Push,' the doctor reminded Isabel.

'If I had mentioned the name "Michael" you would have scolded me. But when Lydia says it, you find nothing wrong with it,' Diana argued.

'Shush, both of you!' Catherine reprimanded them. 'This is not the time or the place.'

'Thank you, Catherine,' Isabel said quite exhausted, her brow dripping with sweat, her cheeks puffy and red with all the effort of pushing

'Besides, if Thomas knew I was in labour he would have done exactly what Michael did. I am certain,' Catherine remarked and Isabel rolled her eyes.

'Thomas was giving a speech. You shouldn't have been in that political gathering in the first place,' Lydia said, an edge to her voice, upset.

'I insisted on going,' Catherine answered back.

'I can't believe you are fighting over this while I'm giving birth to my first born,' Isabel said and gave one more strong push, screaming at the top of her lungs.

The baby came and its cry filled the room. Isabel fell back exhausted. Catherine dried Isabel's sweat with a damp muslin cloth; her forehead, her cheeks, her neck and Lydia kissed her hand congratulating her.

'It's a girl!' The doctor announced and Isabel's eyes filled with tears. She reached out and held her beautiful baby.

'Can I turn now?' Diana asked.

'No stay as you are a little longer. There is still blood everywhere,' Catherine said and she winked at Lydia and Isabel who laughed.

Nathan had been pacing back and forth. In every scream he would halt and look at the door scared, excited, expectant.

'Courage my friend,' John said. 'It is very close now.'

'I don't understand. I hear Isabel screaming one moment, and then the next, there is laughter. What is happening in there?' Nathan asked perplexed.

'Laughter is a good sign. All is well,' Thomas offered and he tapped a gentle rhythm on Nathan's shoulder. He, then, checked the clock on the fireplace. 'I hate to miss this, but I have to be in parliament in half an hour. Catherine will kill me for missing one more labour. She is still so mad for missing our child's birth.'

'Go, don't worry. I will talk to my sister,' John said.

A few minutes later, they heard the baby's cry and Nathan sighed with relief.

'Is my baby sister here?' Tina asked, poking her head into the corridor from behind her half-opened bedroom door.

'I told you not to come in here, Tina,' Nathan said, and he scooped her up with a smile. 'Listen!' he said, and they both heard the baby crying.

'I can't wait to hold her. I had a lot of practise with my dolls,' Tina said happily.

Catherine, Lydia and the doctor, just then, stepped outside the room.

'It's a girl!' Catherine exclaimed and Tina raised her hands above her head.

'Yes! I knew it,' she celebrated.

'My love. Could you please call your brother?' Nathan asked and Tina ran frantically outside calling Tommy's name.

'Go inside,' Lydia said to Nathan, quite moved. 'They are waiting for you.'

Nathan walked hurriedly inside. Isabel, calm and glowing already cradled their baby to her breast and Nathan felt a sudden weakness in his legs. He dropped down next to Isabel but then, he noticed Diana still standing at the corner of the room facing the wall.

'Isabel, what is Diana doing there?'

'I completely forgot,' she said with a chuckle. 'Diana, my dear! All is done now. You can turn round.'

'Finally!' Diana said and she hurried out of the room.

'Don't you want to see the baby first?' Isabel asked.

'Later. I am bursting.'

Isabel and Nathan laughed and then, kissed tenderly. The baby, her pure white skin and short blonde hair, nestled in her mother's breast, was a picture to behold forever.

'It feels like a dream,' Isabel said with tears in her eyes. 'The doctor said she is perfect, and he has confirmed with confidence we can have more children if we wish to.'

The soft knock on the door interrupted them. Tommy and Tina walked reluctantly into the room.

'Come closer. Come meet your sister,' Nathan urged them and both children tiptoed towards Isabel's bed.

'Is she sleeping?' Tina asked, stretching her neck to have a better look.

'Yes, she has just fallen asleep.'

'What is her name?' Tommy asked and Isabel looked at Nathan in wonder.

'The truth is we have never discussed a name,' Isabel admitted.

'What do you think we should call her?' Nathan asked.

'How about Lilly? Tommy offered. 'I have been dreaming of a big field full of lilies all night yesterday. It was the most peaceful and beautiful place I have ever seen in my life. I was so happy there.'

'Lilly, welcome to our family,' Isabel said and she kissed the baby's forehead.

Witney, A year later

Their decision to move to Witney was the best they had made. Isabel instantly fell in love with the place; she loved walking past the working mills and getting to know the local people who were exactly as Nathan described them, kind hearted and warm. They all embraced her family at once, paying them visits and inviting them to all local festivities and social occasions. Isabel felt immediately safe and welcomed and the least she could do was to support the local trades people by buying linen, blankets and furniture for her children's bedrooms and for her school.

Nathan's sister was a treasure too. Carolina and her husband kindly opened up their warm home and welcomed them with no hint of displeasure despite the sudden intrusion of Isabel's and Nathan's large family to their routine. Carolina's own children, Bella and Ron, though older in years than Tina and Tommy, took it upon themselves to make them feel comfortable, played with them and entertained them, sharing their toys and books.

Moreover, Carolina stayed true to her promise to help Isabel with the newborn as Isabel refused to allot the care of her daughter to a nursery maid especially during the first few weary sleepless months. Isabel never complained and she only wished for one thing: to embrace her baby lovingly, smell her hair and kiss her for comfort whenever baby Lilly was unsettled. Though exhausted most days, Isabel never missed the opportunity to spend time with her husband, Tina and Tommy.

She cherished their walks in the vast forest surrounding their estate with the earthy brown and yellow hues, leaves rustling and birds singing the only disturbances to the otherwise pure serenity of the beautiful landscape. Their long strolls ended in Nathan's favourite clearing where there was a small pond always stocked with fish, their scales sparkling as they caught the sun's rays through the dappled water. The children would stand at its edge counting the fish as they swam between the reeds and knotweed; excitement in their shrieks as they saw the air bubbles rising through the shallow of the water before then spotting the dancing fish as they swam closer to the water's surface.

They laid their picnic blanket, another local buy, under

the shade of an old oak tree to enjoy some freshly baked cakes, bread and fruit while chattering and laughing to each other's jokes. And immediately after, Nathan and Tommy fished, sitting patiently with their little rods and tiny nets, while Isabel and Tina, lying next to each other, read books together. Such little, simple moments brought peace to Isabel's soul.

Isabel was especially proud of Tommy who had changed into a different person ever since they moved to Witney a year ago. He was no longer a timid boy. He was bursting with new-found confidence and a charmingly quick wit and had made new friends in no time. Everybody looked up to him, thus, he had no trouble convincing this group of local children to participate in his play.

Nathan and Tommy had worked together writing the play in secret never revealing any details to Isabel and Tina who were eager with curiosity. Thus, to this day, Isabel was still in the dark.

Her tummy churned with excitement and anticipation to see both her adopted children performing and she took her seat in the front row.

'Ladies, gentlemen and children of Witney welcome to our play. Today, you're going to witness the mysterious and breathtaking adventure of the most courageous and fearless five. Two valorous boys and three lionhearted girls are going to enter the gates of a magic kingdom hoping to find the enchanted stone that will bring back the light to their cursed, dark land and restore peace. In their pursuit, they will face ruthless enemies and spine-chilling dragons,' Nathan announced in a thunderous voice.

He held Lilly, his wriggling one-year-old daughter in his arms. Lilly looked absolutely beautiful in her white frilly dress, wearing a wreath of wildflowers in her blonde hair. She resembled a mythical fairy as she shyly buried her face in her father's neck. Every now and then she lifted her head to look in the direction of Tommy and Tina, her brother and sister, who were standing at the back of the stage. They waved at her smiling and pulling funny faces much to her giggly delight. She smiled back and hid again in the warmth of her father's embrace, flapping her little legs impatiently.

Nathan, then, raised his hand and invited the young actors forward and amongst the animated clapping and cheering of the audience, he walked briskly off stage taking his seat next to his wife. Isabel's cheeks had started aching from smiling widely and with such pride while admiring her family on the raised wooden platform which represented the group's theatre stage.

Nathan had ordered its construction from the local carpenters and had paid handsomely for it to be ready and in situ for the day of the grand performance. Lilly held her hands out towards Isabel.

'Mama,' she cooed like a chick and Isabel pulled her onto her lap. Lilly leaned her little head to her mother's bosom comfortably and closed her eyes. She was falling asleep after all the excitement. Isabel was tempted to keep her awake to watch her older siblings perform but on the other hand she knew that her young hellion needed her rest. She sat back relaxing her body against her chair, readying herself to enjoy the performance without having to juggle the spirited little girl in her lap.

The performance of "The Dragon Tamers" had been the most anticipated event for the people of the small rural community of Witney. Isabel noticed how Nathan rubbed his hands and took a deep breath as silence fell like a blanket of fresh snow across the audience and the young actors took their places on stage.

'Are you nervous, my love?' Isabel whispered in Nathan's ear.

'I am,' he whispered back not taking his glittering eyes off the stage.

Isabel, in admiration for this kind man who she loved so deeply, held his hand tightly; 'It will be amazing!' she enthused.

'I know, I've seen the rehearsal. All the children worked so hard. Tommy was a true professional giving directions and performing himself. But still…' Nathan confessed.

My children. She thought and smiled broadly. She could never have hoped for such happiness in her life. Engrossed in the play, Isabel didn't realise how fast her heart was pumping. Baby Lilly, as if having sensed her mother's overwhelming emotions, woke up, looked around and, rubbing her little eyes, craned her neck when she realised her brother and her sister were on stage. She waved and called out 'Tina!' but luckily her sister didn't lose her focus and kept on performing despite the scattered giggles of those who had witnessed Lilly's affectionate call.

Isabel could swear it was the best play she had ever watched. The dialogue was witty and fun evoking the laughter of the audience and the spontaneous claps and cheers in the midst of the play. And in the fighting scenes where duels were played out, with accuracy and seriousness, everybody remained silent but there were gasps of ooh and argh when the young actors swung their swords against the fierce dragons with beautifully choreographed moves.

Nathan smiled proudly during the whole show and nodded reassuringly every time his eyes met Tommy's on stage. And when the play ended the young actors received a standing ovation that lit up their faces. The merriment surrounding the success of the play turned into a festivity for the rural community. The village vicar played the violin and his daughter sang with a voice of an angel while all attendees, hand in hand danced in circles around them.

Isabel joined in too with her three children but after dancing until her cheeks were red with the heat of the exertion, she looked round for Nathan only to realise he was not there.

She turned her head in search of him and spied him talking to a servant while skimming over what seemed to be a note in his hands. Nathan's eyebrows were furrowed. He, then, looked in her direction, as if sensing her eyes on him, and looked away. He pressed his lips into a thin line while rubbing his chin.

Isabel's stomach tensed. She sensed that the news was not good. She broke away and walked briskly to Nathan. He passed her the note and Isabel hurryingly read through the lines. Bile climbed up her throat. Catherine's husband, Thomas, was missing. His ship never made it to the New York port. Isabel drew her breath and with a trembling hand she crumbled the paper. She looked pleadingly at her husband, tears welling behind her eyes.

'Nathan,' she said.

Nathan squeezed her hand lightly into his.

'I know… I have made arrangements. We are all leaving for London in two days,' he said.

THE END

Acknowledgements

My deepest thanks to my Alexandra Z, whose feedback helped me improve my work.

Special thanks to my agent and editor Soulla Christodoulou, who made all this possible.

Author Bio

Electra holds a BA in English Literature and she is an avid romance reader. She had never felt inspired to write until she came across the Regency Romance Novel genre. Since then, she has been seriously hooked. Electra's stories are about strong women who make their way in the world celebrating their womanhood and sensuality. Her motto is 'prepare to fall in love'.

Connect with Electra, she loves to speak to her readers:

X: @electra_tanny
INSTAGRAM: Instagram.com/electra_tanny
EMAIL: electratanny@gmail.com
WEBSITE: www.electratannyromance.com

**Escape into The Dauntless Ladies Series
by Electra Tanny**

John, the Duke of Rutland, was rarely surprised. But one morning, he lay in bed staring at his ceiling, contemplating the most absurd proposal from Oscar, his friend, he had ever heard: 'I want you to sleep with Lydia.'

Never in his wildest dreams would a husband propose, and then thank him for agreeing, to have intercourse with his wife. Not that this was likely to happen. Lydia would never agree to such an arrangement. He was certain a message would promptly arrive from her telling him to stay away and that it was all a sham.

Deep down though, he dared to entertain a wisp of hope; maybe it would be true, the woman of his dreams finally in his arms.

Chapter One

Nottinghamshire 1800

'Oscar, stop pulling your wife's hair!' the Marquess of Eastwood quipped causing giggles and titters to his guests, Earl Clement, and his wife. Oscar looked at his father pouting, trying to understand the meaning of his jest. He then looked at the little green-eyed girl sitting on the floor and reached out to him with open arms. Oscar winced. He didn't like her. Not at all, because ever since she had been born, she got all the attention and praise. How clever she was, how beautiful, how perfect! And to his dismay Oscar had to endure her presence almost every day as their fathers were the best of friends since childhood and with their properties abutting.

'Arrrg,' Oscar growled at the baby girl.

He then stuck his tongue out, turned his back on her and folded his arms in front of his chest. He couldn't stand the sight of her. She, however, crawled towards him and tried to stand up by grabbing his leg. Oscar stood still, waiting for Lady Clement, her mother, to scold her. She should be able to see that she was annoying him, he thought. But, alas, she did not.

'Oh, look at her standing on her feet! How remarkable!' he heard his mother, Lady Eastwood, saying cheerfully.

'What a clever girl!' his father exclaimed.

Oscar got angry and he abruptly moved away causing baby Lydia to collapse tummy first on the floor.

'Oh my!' Lady Clement cried and sprang to her feet in trepidation.

'Oscar! What did you do?' his mum scolded him.

But Lydia was not upset much to everyone's relief. She looked at Oscar. She pulled herself on all fours and crawled after him again.

Lydia did not give up no matter how much Oscar ignored her or even hurt her sometimes. She persisted and in time, as they grew older, Oscar and Lydia became inseparable with an intensity that could be described as need. Every morning, they sat side by side in Oscar's school room because he refused to have any lessons without Lydia. And then, they spent the rest of the day playing together and roaming the countryside. Dolls were quickly discharged from Lydia's playroom; instead, Lydia followed Oscar's lead and she climbed trees, shot arrows, and played all the games Oscar desired. They always returned home covered in mud and Lydia's dresses were almost daily torn.

'Mother, why can't I wear breeches like Oscar? I hate these frilly dresses. They always get in my way!' Lydia argued and fidgeted much to her maid's dismay who tried to remove her destroyed garment without smearing mud on the floor.

'Lydia, you are a girl, my dear!' Her mother answered sternly.

'Well, that's unfair! I will never be able to defeat Oscar

in racing,' Lydia said, stomping her feet.

'I shall not hear it, Lydia. That is enough!' her mother said and stormed out of Lydia's bedroom frustrated.

Later, that evening Lydia wisely did not join her parents for dinner knowing that her mother had a long list of mischief to report to her father. She just leaned against the closed dining room doors eavesdropping and biting her nails. She was not in the habit of spying on her parents, but Lydia's instincts told her that something vile was about to happen. In her nine years, she had never seen her mother that disheartened before. She could hear her mother's anxious pace.

'What is it, my love?' Lydia heard her father asking.

'Lydia is growing into a wildering. What shall we do, my Lord?'

'Oscar seems to like it,' Lydia's father answered, sounding unaffected by his wife's concern.

'Oscar is a lonely boy and Lydia is his only friend. Lydia is all he needs for now but as they grow older, I am afraid she will lack the feminal charm. I doubt Oscar will ever come to regard her as a comely spouse, no matter how much you and Lord Eastwood desire our children betrothal.'

That drew Lord Clement's attention.

'But she is a beauty, is she not?'

'Beauty and feminal charm are not concurrent, my lord. I believe when the time comes, we should allow Lydia to have a season to polish her manners.'

'Too risky. What if she fancies herself in love with a gallant? How would we deter her from such a belief without igniting her resentment?'

Lady Clement fell silent for a minute and Lydia's

stomach tightened with anxiety.

'Then mayhap, Lydia could join a seminary. In fact, her cousins are joining one in a few days.'

'I shall not!' Lydia cried bursting into the room, startling her parents. 'I am not going anywhere!' she hissed to her mother.

'Lydia! Were you eavesdropping?' her mother exclaimed, 'You see now my Lord what I have to endure daily!'

'Your mother is right, my dear. You need to mind your manners. You are not a peasant girl. Your family is an esteemed member of the ton. You need to behave as such!' her father scolded her.

Lydia had heard all this before, and she usually rebuffed her parents' admonition by screaming at them that she would rather be a farmer's daughter. But this time she didn't feel the same violent resentment. She felt fear. What if Oscar would not want to marry her? Was that even a possibility? She could recall the numerous times she heard the Earl and the Marquess in this very room hailing the prospect of merging the two families' legacies and vast fortunes. Maybe, her mother was right she admitted to herself, and her gut squeezed. She returned in her bedroom defeated and that night she hardly slept trying to imagine spending her days away from Oscar. It was unfathomable.

Early the next morning Lydia slipped outside without even breaking her fast to go and find Oscar. She needed his advice. She was certain her wise friend would have a far better proposal than her parents who insisted on sending her away to become a 'lady'. What a ridiculous notion. Oscar would laugh in tears if he heard her parents' silly aspiration.

She took a short cut through the muddy fields instead of following the stone-paved path to the creek where she was to meet him. She knew that her shoes and the rim of her dress were doomed to destruction, and she would get in trouble for it. But really, she couldn't think of a worse punishment than what her parents had already decided for her. She ran fast until her lungs started burning but she only stopped when she reached the little hill she and Oscar rolled down on wet, muddy days like this. She smiled to herself thinking that she would challenge Oscar to a sliding competition on their way back later. She looked down at her dress. It was already soaked at the edges and some of the frills were hanging loose. Lydia bit her bottom lip thinking of her mother's angry face but then she dismissed the thought and just shrugged her shoulders. She hated this dress anyway.

She rushed away passing by the line of walnut trees that she and Oscar climbed daily. She used to get injured quite often in the past, scraping her knees, or suffering splinters deep in her skin that her mother patiently removed every time but not anymore. She could proudly say that she was one of the best climbers, after Oscar, of course.

A few minutes later, she was finally able to see the creek and luckily Oscar was already there. Seeing her friend baiting their fishing rods, filled her heart with sadness. Tears started welling behind her eyes, but she had to stay calm. Oscar would know what to do to escape her dreadful fate.

The sound of the crunching pebbles attracted Oscar's attention, he turned to look at her.

'Lydia, good, you are here. What's wrong? Were you

crying?' he asked anxiously.

'My parents! They are making me go away!' Lydia said disheartened.

'Go where?'

'To a girl's seminary,' she said, throwing her hands in the air.

Oscar lowered his head and kicked a stone in the creek. 'You know Lydia, go! I don't need you anyway!' he shouted, his face turning red and then, he ran off.

Lydia stayed behind looking at her friend fleeing, quite shocked. How could he leave her like that now that she needed him the most? She tightened her grips and puffed through her nose. *Coward*, she heard herself saying but she immediately reconsidered. No Oscar was not a coward; he hadn't abandoned her. He was just upset by the news. Lydia was certain that he would look for her later that afternoon. In fact, he might already be on his way to her home. She was certain that a good sprint would help him clear his head and see his folly of abandoning her helpless to her parents' designs. She decided to go back home and wait for him.

For three days Lydia waited and waited, wandering the house trying to understand why Oscar had not come. She kept thinking that maybe she should go and find him, but she was reluctant. What if he was mad at her and sent her away. Her heart would break if that was the case. On the fourth day, Oscar, finally, showed up as if nothing had happened. In fact, he was beaming.

'I have the most wonderful news, Lydia.'

Lydia looked at him arching her eyebrow. *Seriously?* she thought. But she let him continue, curious to find out what was causing him so much happiness with her departure only a few days away.

'In a year from now I am going to Eton. Finally, I am going to meet other boys and be able to do the things I have always longed for!'

Lydia felt sick to her stomach. Why would Oscar feel that she was not enough, she wondered. She believed they had the best of times together and she always yielded to Oscar's wishes. Lydia was hurt but seeing Oscar's excitement, she convinced herself to set her ill feelings aside.

'I am so happy for you, Oscar. Do you think you will miss me? I know I will miss you,' Lydia said, blushing.

Oscar shrugged his shoulders.

'I don't think I will have the time to miss you. You know, us boys will have a lot of studies and with my new friends…' Oscar said but then he paused. 'Well, maybe, a little bit,' he admitted, and Lydia's face lit up.

On the day of Lydia's departure, Oscar and his family were, also, present to bid her well along with all the staff of the Clement household who evidently adored the spirited, little girl. Oscar could see Lydia was inconsolable and he wanted to tell her something to make her feel better, but he couldn't think of anything. How odd he thought, and his heart thumped hard thinking of how easy it was for Lydia to console him when he felt miserable. She always had the right words, and he loved his friend for that. He was going to miss her terribly; he knew it well, and he cursed himself for not even admitting that to her.

Oscar lowered his head trying to push back a sob that was blocking his throat. He rubbed his sleeve against his runny nose. He knew he would not be able to hold his tears back and he now wished for Lydia to get in her carriage and be gone as quickly as possible because he was about to make a spectacle of himself.

'Lydia?' Oscar heard Lady Clement querying and he looked up.

Lydia had stopped right in front of the lowered carriage steps and stood still for a few seconds. Then, to everyone's surprise, she whirled round on tiptoe, ran to Oscar and throwing her hands around his neck gave him a quick peck on his cheek. She then ran off again and climbed into the carriage without glancing back at him. Oscar, wide-eyed, touched his cheek with his palm and he felt butterflies in his tummy. He knew that everyone was looking at his raging red face. He was happy and despite seeing the carriage disappearing from his view he resumed his courage. He pulled his shoulders back and walked off feeling both his feet and his heart light. He had nothing to worry about. He might have just lost his only friend, but he had a lot of work to do to prepare himself for Eton. He had decided to be the best student and the best in fencing and in all things boys of his age were expected to be the best at.

Thus, while Oscar was working hard to be the best at everything, Lydia found herself desperately bored in the seminary with no inclination in the art of sewing or drawing and little interest in the principals of feminine propriety. However, she did perfect her piano playing.

'Perhaps, mon petit, there is still hope for you!' Madame Bordeaux, the headmistress of the seminary, commended as Lydia finished exhibiting. Lydia's face reddened and she clenched her fists but her cousin Magda, who sensed her rage, tightened her grip around her arm. 'Lydia, not a word,' she whispered.

Luckily for Lydia, her cousins Magda and Kate always helped her to control her temper. Both girls, extremely intelligent and with their own unique interests, were equally dispassionate about the education they were receiving. However, their overall attitude was one of prudence and pragmatism and both shared a realistic view of the world. They knew what was expected of them and they delivered without complaint.

'Look at that!' Lydia growled, shaking Oscar's latest letter in her hand. 'How lucky Oscar is. He studies Latin, Greek and Maths; meanwhile we are learning frivolities!' she said, pacing back and forth in the bedroom the three girls shared.

Magda quit reading her book and peered over at Lydia.

'Well, who stops you. You can learn Latin if you want to.'

'You know what I mean, Magda! Whatever, we learn we must do so in secret as if committing the gravest sin.'

'Do not complain Lydia. It is what it is,' Magda said, turning the page of her newly acquired astronomy book with the greatest of care.

'I don't like it!' Lydia said as she dived into her bed.

'You should not like it. You must but cope and do the best for yourself. One day our seemingly insignificant endeavours may mean something,' Magda answered pragmatically while pushing her spectacles to the bridge of her nose.

'This story is my best one yet!' Kate exclaimed obviously oblivious of Lydia's and Kate's discussion. 'Lydia, could you read it, please and tell me what you think?'

'Of course, cousin. You know how much I love your stories. Hand your manuscript to me. I shall start immediately!'

At that moment, the three girls listened to hurried steps outside their bedroom door. Magda frantically hid her book under her pillow and Lydia tossed the pages under her bed. The door opened abruptly.

'Ladies! J'ai de bonnes nouvelles pour vous,' said Madam Bordeaux. 'As of today, Master Lorrean shall join our seminary to teach you dance!'

'Oh Madame! C'est mervellieux!' Magda exclaimed.

Kate clapped with enthusiasm. Lydia simply tried to keep a straight face sensing her cousins' feigning excitement; she knew only too well the Page sisters despised any form of swaying and twirling.